PRAISE FOR THE VALE VALLEY SWANS!

"This bundle is just great. Two great little stories with some big surprises that make you just want to squeeeeeeee and go awwwww."

Becca ∼ Love Bytes Reviews

"LOVED Kellan and Vic. I can't wait to read more of their story!"

Goodreads Reviewer

"...A sweet and dear read. Vic was patient and loving, an attribute which served him well with his young and inexperienced swan mate. I adored Kellan's exuberance and lust for life."

Evelise ∼ S.E.X. Reviews

"I'm head over heels for Kellan and Vic. I can totally see myself reading this one again."

Amazon Reviewer

"...As good as this book was, the real prize was watching our little hatchling finally breaking free from its shell. That was the best. I was in tears. It was perfect."

"A Swan for Christmas is a delightfully fun story about a swan shifter who finds love. I love the writing. The character development is well done, and the storyline is entertaining. *A Swan for Christmas and A Hatchling for Valentine's* are a must read when you're looking for something sweet and cute. And shifters. And adorable and charming shifters who will melt your heart."

A SWAN FOR CHRISMAS

&

A HATCHLING FOR VALENTINE'S

A Vale Valley Bundle

FEATURING KELLAN & VIC'S NEW YEAR'S EVE

FROM.
A BUNDLE OF JOY

M.M. Wilde

A SWAN FOR CHRISTMAS

Vale Valley Season 1, Book 4

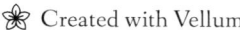

I'd like to give a huge thank you to author Giovanna Reaves for inviting me to be a part of the Vale Valley world that she created. I've grown to love this mysterious, secret town that is a sanctuary to those special beings—whether shifter, magical or from an omegaverse world—who are in need of love and a permanent home. It's been an honor and I hope to tell more Vale Valley stories in the future!

CHAPTER ONE

*K*ellan shivered against the vicious chill of the night air. Snow had fallen in fluffy piles, blanketing the unfamiliar forest in white that sparkled where the moonlight filtered through the tall pines. If he didn't shift back to his swan form soon, he would die.

So far, he'd been able to complete the change every five minutes or so, then warm up for about an hour before he would abruptly change back again. But even though he didn't have a way to tell time, the ability to shift again still eluded him and he was sure he'd been in his human form for at least ten minutes already.

Why is this happening to me?

While shifting back and forth too many times in a row could make the process difficult until sufficient time had passed—which allowed the energy reserves to build back up—he'd never experienced a situation where he couldn't *stop* himself from shifting. His intention had been to stay a swan for as long as possible so he wouldn't freeze to death.

Until I figure out what I'm going to do.

But none of that mattered in the face of getting out of the elements in the next few minutes. His future would no longer be an issue if he was dead.

Kellan bit back the rising tears as he vigorously scrubbed his arms in a futile attempt to warm up. He stood on a patch of moss under the boughs of an enormous pine but could no longer jog in place to keep his circulation going. When he'd fallen from the truck he'd been traveling in with his herd, he'd hurt his ankle and it had begun to swell. Although the large tree kept him sheltered somewhat from the wind, and he wasn't standing right in the snow, he was still freezing his ass off.

He closed his eyes, concentrating with all his might, pressing his lips together in a tight line as he struggled to initiate the shift. Kellan let out a helpless whimper. No tingle. No heat simmering beneath his skin. No warning ache in his joints. Nothing.

I'm going to die.

Kellan gasped at the loud snap of a branch. He curled in on himself as he frantically glanced around to discover the source of the noise, his swan at the forefront of his mind as if he was about to shift, even though it no longer seemed possible. His eyes went wide and he covered his mouth with the back of his hand in terror.

Wolf!

Even though he knew he was close to dying anyway, being torn to pieces by a wolf would be so much more horrible than slowly descending into darkness.

The massive beast advanced toward him then paused when it came to the edge of the small river right across from Kellan. He'd been using the narrow waterway to travel on whenever he'd been in swan form, hoping it would eventually lead him somewhere he could seek shelter. But the minimal expanse of water wouldn't be large enough to save him from being eaten by the wolf. The hulking animal with a thick brown and grey coat wouldn't be stopped by such a paltry barrier. One hearty leap would place him right in fang and claw range of Kellan.

Kellan jumped then yelped, his feet sliding out from under him, his ass hitting the ground as the wolf instantly changed into a tall, rugged man with solid, corded muscles filling his frame. The man's gaze bore into Kellan, his eyes still retaining the left-over glow of his wolf. He struck Kellan as being like a lumberjack or hunter. In addition to his hunky body, he wore a long beard, had bushy eyebrows and his hair hung long over one side of his face.

Or maybe he's just a hipster. The man was also as naked as Kellan was.

"What are you doing out here like that? You'll freeze to death!" Despite no longer being in wolf form, the stranger easily made the leap across the river.

Kellan's body shook so hard from the cold, his teeth chattering so violently, that he was unable to form words in response. But the man didn't seem concerned about waiting to hear what he had to say. Instead, he scooped him up, jumped back over the water and jogged at a fast clip through the woods.

He's so warm.

His initial instinct had been to fight and struggle, but where would he go? What would he do? He was doomed if he didn't accept the stranger's help.

Kellan snuggled against the firm, muscled chest of the man, his heat and scent so comforting. *Safe.* Surely, his swan would protest if he were in danger? Kellan tensed. Then again, his swan hadn't been working so well for the past few hours. *I need to stay on guard.* When it wasn't even safe to trust his own family, how could it possibly be a wise move to trust a stranger?

"Here we go. Let's get you warmed up."

The man slowed as he approached an older pick-up truck with red paint fading in spots and supported by giant snow tires.

The lone streetlamp that lit up the gravel-covered parking area was just enough for Kellan to get a vague idea of his surroundings. The man yanked open the passenger side door, shoved a pile of clothing aside, then set Kellan down on the seat. The moment he was released by the stranger, the sharp bite of cold surrounded him again and he noted that the stranger seemed to be in the same predicament. The man rubbed his hands together as he darted around the front of the cab then got in on the other side.

Once he was inside, Kellan's would-be rescuer fired up the engine and let the heat blast. He remained silent as he dug through the clothing.

"Take this." The man held out a red and black flannel shirt to Kellan.

Kellan accepted it, not wanting to look up. *To act like I'm as good as him.* Finn would always berate him if he slipped up and made eye contact.

"T-thank you."

Kellan shrugged on the shirt, buttoning it with trembling fingers as the truck gradually warmed. He chanced a peek at the stranger, trying not to stare brazenly at his cock when he lifted his ass out of the seat to tug his jeans on.

He doesn't have any underwear on. Kellan lowered his eyes again, his cheeks heating. He'd never seen such a handsome, hunky man before. None of his swan herd were built that way. Kellan held the fabric of the soft cotton shirt to his nose, inhaling the masculine, gorgeous scent. It was like pine mixed with spice and musk. Never had anything been so alluring to him—which was odd—since they were different shifter species. But then again, Kellan had never met a wolf before, so he wasn't sure what they were supposed to smell like. Maybe they all had an amazing scent. Wolves certainly seemed very popular amongst shifters.

Unlike swans.

"Take these, too." The man shoved a pair of brown socks at

him. "I'm worried about your toes. You can get frostbite a lot quicker than you'd think."

As Kellan started to yank one of them on, he tugged a bit too hard on his bad ankle. "Ow!"

"Are you hurt?"

The man sounded very worried.

"I... I fell. Twisted my ankle."

Kellan peered up at him, he couldn't help himself. His curiosity had gotten him into plenty of trouble over the years, but he wanted to see the stranger, *needed* to know what he was thinking, if he was annoyed with Kellan or truly as concerned as he seemed.

Oh...

The man was even more handsome now that he could get a good look at him inside the lighted cab.

"Lemme see."

Kellan held up his foot for inspection, peeling the top of the sock back enough for an appraisal. The man frowned as he checked it, lightly poking it where there was some swelling at the ankle bone. Kellan hissed.

"Is that tender?"

Kellan nodded. "Yeah."

"Okay." He lowered Kellan's leg, and the same as it had been when he'd set Kellan down in the truck, he felt the loss of the man's touch somewhere deep inside. "It doesn't appear too bad, I'm thinking you've got a mild sprain. When we get back to the inn, I'll get you a wrap for it." He twisted his body around then plucked a fluffy down jacket from behind the front bench seat, then presented it to Kellan. "Put this on too. I don't know how long you were out there like that, but I'm thinking it was lucky I came along when I did."

Kellan's stomach roiled as he held the coat in front of him, not wanting it to touch his skin. The man's scent was there, but so was another one. A sickening one. "I don't want you to think I'm ungrateful, but..." He wrinkled his nose. "This is filled with smelly old dead feathers!"

The stranger furrowed his brow, his elbow draped over the steering wheel as he considered Kellan. "I don't understand. It's filled with goose down. Are you allergic?"

Kellan gasped then threw the garment, the jacket smacking the man in the face. He sputtered and choked then pulled it away, clutching it in his lap as he frowned at Kellan again.

Oh dear. Already I'm making him not like me.

"What was that for?"

"I'm sorry! But those are my cousins' feathers! I mean, not my *actual* cousins, probably, but I don't know where they came from or how they got there. If they were being used outside in a nest with the fresh air, that would be one thing, but they're suffocating in that synthetic fabric."

A smile tugged at the corner of the man's mouth and Kellan huffed. He didn't see what was so amusing.

"Now I understand why I found you out in the Vale woods. You're a goose shifter who needs a home."

Kellan crossed his arms and huffed again. "I am not a goose shifter. I'm a *swan*."

The still-shirtless man ran his gaze down Kellan's body then met his eyes. "A very lovely swan." He dipped his chin. "My apologies." He angled his body around, but this time when he retrieved something from behind the seat, it was a red, wool blanket. "Do you have any sheep cousins?"

Kellan was working up to a snit, but he caught a slight twitch at the corner of the man's mouth. He chuckled. "Not that I know of." Kellan ducked his head. "Thank you. You've been so nice to me, saved my life. I didn't mean to snap at you."

"It's okay, don't you worry about that." The man's voice had softened. "Why don't you wrap that around yourself, though." He adjusted the thick cover over Kellan's shoulders and gathered it so the blanket covered his bare legs. "There. That's better." The man offered him a smile. "How about I introduce myself? I'm Vic, the Alpha of a very small pack and owner of the Vale Valley Inn and Restaurant. And you?"

He held out his hand and Kellan let his smaller one be swallowed up by it. After two quick pumps, he released him. As it had been with every other touch from Vic, Kellan was sorry it was over.

"Nice to meet you, Vic. I'm Kellan, and as you now know, a swan shifter." Kellan chewed on his bottom lip. "You mentioned your inn. I don't have any money, or anything at all, to offer you in payment. But I work very hard and I could pay you back if I could stay there for a few days? I'll even give you double what I owe."

Vic shook his head and Kellan's stomach sank. *Oh no. Now what do I do?*

"You don't need to pay me, Kellan. I'm sure I can find something for you to do around the inn or restaurant if you want to help out. My inn tends to be a place where a lot of the new residents start out when they first arrive. Some stay on and work there, others find the place in town where they were meant to be. For them, the inn is merely a stepping stone to where they belong in Vale Valley."

"Wow." Kellan tilted his head. "Is there something special about Vale Valley? It sounds as though there are a lot of shifters here and people who have nowhere else to go."

Vic tugged at his beard, his brow wrinkling. "Yeah, that's about right. Vale Valley is where a lot of us ended up because we were drifting. The town's origins are with the Vale family, but there are also a large variety of shifters, Alphas and omegas and even dragons and witches. But we all watch out for each other, keep each other's secrets from the prying eyes of the rest of the world."

Kellan's eyes rounded, and he clutched the blanket tighter around him. He glanced around, but all he could see were the black silhouettes of the trees. "Dragons and witches? Do they eat the residents or cast evil spells?"

Vic choke-snorted, then seemed to get hold of himself. "No, little Kellan. Like any town, there have been some unsavory characters, but our residents are all good souls. Even the dragons and witches." Vic winked. "I can't think of another place I'd rather be."

Kellan considered Vic's words along with how protected being with the big wolf made him feel. *And he's even an Alpha. Wow.* "Vale Valley does sound like a special town. Do you think I'll be allowed to stay? I can keep secrets, too."

"I have a feeling you were led to us, Kellan." Vic smiled then put the truck in gear. As he reversed out of the parking area, bunches of snow kicking up behind his tires, he gave Kellan a quick pat on the shoulder. "That's how it usually works. I'll have Rosemary Vale, the town mayor, stop by the restaurant tomorrow. If you still want to stay in the Valley, she can add you to the population records."

"Then I would belong in the town?"

Vic shifted gears then pulled onto the small plowed road. "Yes, you would belong."

Kellan sniffed back the emotion burning in his throat. Maybe he *could* have people in his life who truly cared about him and who didn't think he was worthless.

Maybe I can have a real home.

CHAPTER TWO

*V*ic glanced sideways at the unexpected find in his passenger seat. On occasion, a newcomer would be drawn to the town, most of the arrivals unknowingly following their gut instinct leading them to their true home. But this was the first time he'd been personally involved in such an event.

"We're almost there."

Kellan peered up at him. "The town is so quiet. But it's very pretty. I don't like cities or anywhere too crowded or noisy."

Vic grinned. *Definitely led here.* "Then this'll be your kind of place."

He found it interesting that Kellan was a swan shifter. He'd never met any avian shifters before. If there were any in Vale Valley, he wasn't aware of them. Swans were such beautiful creatures—he'd always admired the graceful and majestic birds. Even some of the rooms at the Inn had paintings of swans on the walls. Mateo, one of his buddies and the town's tattoo artist, had done some excellent pen and ink drawings of swans for him. *Those* he kept in his private cabin on the inn's premises.

Yes. Interesting that I should be the one to find him.

Yet, that seemed to be the way of the town's magic. Somehow, the circumstances had been put in place that he would be taking his nightly run in the same area Kellan was in trouble. Vic assumed it was why his heart had been thundering upon his first touch of Kellan and why he'd been so reluctant to let him go. Somewhere deep inside he must have recognized Kellan was a swan.

That's all it was. Nothing else.

"I'm sorry if I ruined your plans tonight." Kellan's voice held a tinge of worry. "I know I can be a bother at times, but I'll do my best not to cause any trouble."

Vic drew his eyebrows together as he clutched the wheel tighter. "I hardly think almost dying in the cold was done to intentionally disrupt my evening." He snorted. "And anyway, there was nothing to disrupt. I never have much going on outside of operating the inn and restaurant." Vic shifted in his seat. *Don't need to sound too pathetic.* He doubted the swan cared how non-existent his social life was. "Here we are."

Vic pulled up to the curb in the registration only zone at the entrance of the inn. An A-line structure made up the front of the motel that housed the lobby, with the restaurant to the left. Everything was done in pine wood and conveyed an old-fashioned, rustic charm which was what he'd been aiming for ten years before when he'd first had it built from the ground up.

He placed the truck in park then turned to Kellan. "Wait here where it's warm and I'll see what staff rooms are available." Vic offered Kellan what he hoped was a reassuring smile. "Maybe there's one with a view of the lake."

Kellan smiled back, and a rush of warmth filled Vic's heart. He quickly averted his gaze as heat bloomed under his cheeks and his cock stirred in interest. It had been so long since he'd gotten laid that the sight of the luscious creature in his truck had him unusually flustered.

He's in trouble. He doesn't need you creeping up on him, you old horndog.

Maybe thirty-two wasn't that old, but compared to the young thing seated next to him, it suddenly seemed ancient. He cleared his throat. "Be right back."

Before Kellan could respond, Vic rushed to the entrance and grabbed the handle to one of the double glass doors and swung it wide. He noted that Mark, the guest relations clerk on duty, had salted the walkway outside and was in the process of placing yellow caution signs to warn patrons that the stone flooring might be slippery.

Vic winced as a thought struck him. Mark was an initiate in the local coven, so perhaps he wouldn't introduce him to Kellan right away. While Vic knew Mark was a cool guy, Kellan might still be afraid the Vale Valley witches would cast an evil spell on him.

"Hey, Mark. Has it been busy?"

Mark glanced up. "Hi, Vic. No, super slow. I think this snow-storm has kept people away. I've been trying to stay occupied as best I can."

Vic strolled over to the reception desk opposite the entrance, then glanced at the brass keys hanging on the wall behind it. No keycards for his place—too much in the way of modern stuff didn't do it for him.

"Yeah. I figured. Enjoy it while it lasts. In a couple weeks, the Thanksgiving melee will ensue. Then you'll be *wishing* no one was here."

Mark chuckled. "Probably. It gets crazy?"

The witch-initiate had only been working there for a short while. He hadn't even experienced the summer rush yet.

"Yeah. There's only here—and now the Dozing Dragon Bed and Breakfast—for all the relatives coming to visit during the holi-days." Vic narrowed his eyes as he perused the available rooms.

"Listen, I have a shifter out in the truck who needs a place to stay. I'm grabbing 217 if you want to make a note that it's been taken."

Mark came around the counter then woke up the computer. "Sure thing. Wolf?"

Vic tried to hold back what he was sure would be a telling smile. "Nah, swan."

Mark arched his eyebrows. "Wow. I don't know any swan shifters. Can't wait to meet him."

"Yeah... about that." Vic rubbed the back of his neck. "He's a bit nervous about witches, thinks they'll cast evil spells on him. I'm sure he'll be fine once he discovers you're a good guy. Just don't get your feelings hurt if he acts strange around you."

"That's cool." Mark shrugged. "He doesn't have much to worry about from me right now, anyway." He smirked. "Even if I was inclined to, I'm not at that level yet."

Vic enjoyed having the attractive, dark-haired young man working for him. He got along great with the rest of the staff and was reliable and efficient. He doubted it would ever happen, but he'd welcome the chance to take him on fulltime.

"You'll do great, hang in there." Vic glanced over his shoulder. "Better get my charge into his new room. He was half frozen when I found him."

"Oh no. Yeah, I'll see you later then."

Vic dipped his chin once in response then headed back to the truck. He'd left the engine running to keep Kellan warm, but he imagined the poor thing was exhausted and hungry.

I wonder what his story is?

After climbing inside the cab, Vic steered the truck to the other side of the restaurant then around back to the main building of the inn. Kellan's room was toward the end and would offer the promised view of the lake. He hoped to make him as comfortable as possible, so Kellan could work through whatever it was he needed to in order to build a new life.

Vic parked next to the elevator, but since Kellan only wore socks and he wasn't sure how bad off his ankle was, he'd planned on carrying him upstairs anyway. He dropped out of the truck and by the time he'd made it around to the passenger side, Kellan already had the door open and was trying to climb down, his pale, thin legs hanging out from the bottom edges of the blanket.

"Whoa, hold on." Vic scurried over to scoop him up in his arms. "I've got you."

Kellan pulled the blanket around his face, but still snuggled against Vic's chest anyway. "Thanks."

Vic resisted the bizarre urge to nuzzle Kellan's head and concentrated instead on not slipping on any icy spots. His sensitive nose picked up the same enticing scent it had the first time he'd held Kellan. While he'd remained aware of it in the truck, holding him close had him on edge, itchy under his skin but without a way to scratch it. Kellan smelled of sweetness, of fresh berries and cream or perhaps cotton candy and newly frosted cake. He stifled a groan. None of those things were exactly right, but it didn't prevent the aroma from making him want to bury his nose in Kellan's neck or lick him all over.

"Shit."

Kellan tensed then lifted his head to meet Vic's eyes. "What's wrong?"

Vic's eyes widened. *Did I say that out loud?* "Oh, uh... I forgot to grab a first aid kit at the front desk for your ankle." *Quick save and not even close to being a lie.* "But I can get room service to bring one up."

The elevator door opened, and Vic stepped inside. Kellan rested his head against his shoulder again and Vic wondered what had his wolf so worked up about the swan, why he found the young man so alluring. While different shifter species mated all the time, some of them even pairing up with humans, he'd never experienced such an immediate or strong pull from someone. Hell, he'd been with a couple of bears and even a squirrel once—which his wolf buddies still teased him about—but he hadn't wanted to hold onto them and keep them safe forever.

Vic gulped as they reached the second floor and he remained rooted in place as the doors opened, his random musings like a gut punch.

Oh hell no. Impossible. He'd given up on finding his fated wolf omega once his pack had almost been wiped from Earth. The rare, deadly virus that had claimed the majority of the pack population, his family included, had forced him to accept that he'd be without his true match. So, how could a swan be his fated mate?

Ridiculous.

He sighed then stepped out of the lift before the doors could close on them again. They reached room 217 and Vic decided to worry about his crazy ideas later. Kellan's wellbeing was all that mattered at the moment.

Once he'd juggled Kellan and the key, he nudged the door open with his toe then stepped inside. The only staff room left with a lake view had a single, queen-sized bed and a small balcony. The comforter—which thankfully didn't contain goose down—was white, with a pattern of watercolor-style evergreens densely grouped at the bottom then thinning out until the top of the covering was solid white. The floor was made of pine, but green throw rugs similar to the ones in the lobby took up the open spaces. An entertainment center with a dresser, a table with two chairs near the glass door leading to the balcony and a kitchenette filled the rest of the room.

Vic carried Kellan to one of the padded chairs, then gently set him down. Their eyes met, and for a moment, Vic held his breath, not wanting to break the connection between them. Kellan stared up at him from chocolate-brown irises, long black lashes framing his wide eyes. His fair skin was almost the same shade as his platinum hair that was longer on top, with soft waves combed to one side.

Vic swallowed hard then carefully disentangled himself from Kellan. Neither of them seemed anxious to let go, but if he didn't release him immediately, he worried he might do something inappropriate and out of character.

"Uh, let me call room service for the kit." Vic searched through the inn's welcome folder until he found the page he wanted. He handed it to Kellan. "Here, pick something out to eat and I'll have them bring that up too."

While Kellan perused the selections, Vic tried not to stare. He went around randomly checking that everything was in place, even though he already knew his staff would have left the room meticulous.

"I'd like a big salad with lots of vegetables, and whatever fish you have. Is that all right?"

Vic whirled around then accepted the menu back from Kellan. "Of course. We should still have some fresh walleye, but if not, the cook will have either catfish or bass." Vic picked up the phone receiver. "We have fresh pies and cakes, too, if you'd like dessert." He figured the guy could use a few extra calories.

Kellan's cheeks flushed. "Nothing like that. But if you have any berries, I would eat those."

"For dessert?" *Yuck.* "Okay, I'll ask. We usually have some frozen ones in the walk-in."

After placing Kellan's order, he requested that someone bring up a first aid kit right away. Once he'd hung up from that he regarded Kellan, who was curled up on the chair with the blanket still wrapped tightly around his body, his legs tucked underneath him. He was gazing out of the window, seemingly at nothing. It was well after eight o'clock and being that they were on the edge of town, not much was visible in the darkened, wooded surroundings.

Vic scratched his chin through his beard. He wasn't sure how much Kellan wanted to talk about what he'd been through or how he'd come to arrive in Vale Valley, and Vic didn't want to pressure him. If Kellan had been led to the Valley, it meant he was supposed to be there. It wasn't up to Vic or anyone else to pry into his business. But that didn't mean that Vic wasn't dying to know everything he could about his swan guest.

A knock on the door jarred him from his thoughts and he rushed to answer it. Dora, the restaurant hostess for the night, handed him the first aid kit. "It's really quiet in the dining room so Mark asked if I'd bring this up now so you don't have to wait. The food should be ready in another fifteen. Oh, and Skip said to tell you he had some walleye left. It was caught this morning."

"Nice. Thanks, Dora."

He closed the door behind her and turned his attention to Kellan. "Hey, if it's all right, I was going to wrap your ankle for you."

Kellan turned away from the window and smiled, yet there was a hint of melancholy to his expression. "It's all right. I'll pay close attention, so I can do it myself next time."

As Vic pulled up a chair and placed it in front of Kellan, he pondered how he might broach the subject of Kellan's circumstances without coming across as too nosy. He unzipped the red bag and pulled out the self-sticking, stretch wrap he needed then gently lifted Kellan's injured ankle and propped it on his thigh. Once he did, Kellan's blanket fell open, exposing his bare leg. Vic tore away his gaze, not only out of respect, but because he didn't need to encourage his filthy mind any further. It was doing quite well on its own, even with Kellan all bundled up.

"Normally, I would have you put ice on this, but I think you've had enough of *that* for one evening. We'll keep it wrapped and after you eat, you can get into bed and keep it elevated." *But not until I'm long gone.* He wasn't about to stick around to tuck Kellan in. There was temptation and then there was torture.

"So... You probably want to be left alone. After your food gets here, I'll give you your privacy." Vic finished binding Kellan's ankle then rose, placing his foot on the chair he'd been sitting in. "I'll grab you a pillow to put under that."

"Thank you." Kellan ducked his head. "I understand if you have to go. I guess you're pretty busy."

Vic straightened. "Huh?" He shook his head. "Hardly. This place is dead right now. I just figured you'd want your rest. Plus, I'm a stranger."

Kellan peered up at him. "You don't have to be." He wiggled in his chair, adjusting his ankle a bit. "Not if you don't want to. I haven't had anyone to talk to in a long time. You could also tell me about the town and what jobs you want me to do." Kellan's smile widened, his sadness no longer evident. "I'm a little tired, but I couldn't sleep right now anyway. I'm too nervous and excited."

"Oh." Vic considered the unexpected turn of events. "In that case, I'll hang out a bit." He smiled back at Kellan. "And feel free to ask anything you want. I'm hoping you'll like it here."

And that you'll stay.

CHAPTER THREE

Kellan wiped his mouth, barely able to finish the last spoonful of blueberries with cream that had been his dessert. Vic was being so good to him. Not constantly staring at and drooling all over the handsome shifter was going to take a lot of effort on his part. He didn't want to wear out his welcome. While Kellan had eaten, Vic had gone downstairs to give the reception clerk a break. He'd just returned, and Kellan didn't miss how his heart had skipped a beat the moment Vic had stepped into the room.

"How was everything?" Vic gestured to the empty plates.

Kellan chuckled. "Everything was wonderful. I promise I didn't finish it all up to be polite."

Vic perched on the end of the bed and folded his hands in front of him. Kellan still had his ankle propped up on the second chair. He pointed to Kellan's foot. "Do you need some painkiller, or is that too tight or anything?"

Kellan picked at the blanket that had gradually pooled to his waist while he'd been eating. The room was more than warm enough and his body had finally gotten back to what seemed to be a normal temperature.

That was too close a call. "I'm fine, thank you." He regarded Vic. "Are you sure I'm not keeping you from anything?"

Vic chuckled. "Trust me. I lead a pretty solitary life." His eyes widened almost imperceptibly, as if he hadn't meant to say that. He plucked his beard. "So... I don't want to pry, but can I ask what you were doing out there like that? What I mean is, why didn't you just shift? I thought swans were accustomed to the cold."

"We are and I tried." Kellan drew his eyebrows together. "Something weird happened, though. After I was pushed out of the truck and left behind, I figured I'd stay shifted until I found somewhere safe or warm." He sighed. "I couldn't really think clearly at all I'm afraid. I was too upset."

A low growl sounded from Vic and Kellan straightened. He tensed as anger twisted Vic's features.

"*Who* pushed you?" Vic bared his teeth and Kellan tugged the blanket around him again, his heart pounding. "I'll make them pay!"

"Oh, uh..." *Why did I mention that?* "I'm sure they're long gone, which is just as well." He lowered his head. "They didn't want me around anyway." Kellan sniffed. "Haven't for a long time."

"Hey." Vic's tone had softened and he moved off the bed, kneeling in front of Kellan. He tilted his head to try and catch Kellan's gaze. "Come on, look at me." Kellan lifted his eyes to meet Vic's. "Sorry I got so worked up, I didn't mean to yell like that. I just..." He sucked in a deep breath before continuing, "I just can't stand the thought of anyone being so cruel to you." Kellan noticed Vic balling his fists. "You could've been injured much worse than you were, or even killed."

Kellan took a chance and placed a hand on Vic's shoulder.

"I've been expecting something like this from them for a while, to be honest. And they were just pulling away from the rest stop when my brother shoved me out of the truck bed."

Vic's fell back on his heels as his jaw dropped. "Your *brother*? Where was the rest of your family when this happened?"

Kellan removed his hand. He didn't want to upset Vic with the gruesome details of his upbringing, but maybe it was time to share what he'd been through with someone who might actually care. Vic seemed as if he did. *What would that be like?* Finn had tried to drill into his head that love was for losers and no one would ever love him anyway. Still, Kellan had held onto hope.

"I don't have any other family. Only Finn, my brother. My parents were killed in a flying accident when they were caught in a blizzard a few years ago. Most of the bevy was lost, it was so horrible. Then there's the rest of my herd, eight of us, including me." Kellan's shoulders slumped. "Well, seven now. And I guess I should stop referring to them as my herd."

Vic settled on the floor at his feet, the large man gazing up at him with compassion. "You're not alone, Kellan, I promise. Vale Valley exists for a reason, to be that shining beacon for those of us who've been cast aside." Vic clasped his hand. "I lost my family too when a deadly virus tore through our pack. But I've found a home and community and have built a good life here. Everyone's going to welcome you with open arms, I promise."

A measure of peace filled him. Vale Valley could only be a million times better than living with his rotten brother or any of the other vicious members of his herd. *Ex-herd.* Kellan smiled.

"Thank you for everything, Vic. Especially for staying here with me tonight. I've been so lonely for such a long time. They all hated me because I wouldn't steal like them."

Vic's eyebrows shot up. "You're from a herd of thieving swans?"

Heat bloomed under his cheeks. "When I hear it out loud

like that, it's even more humiliating. But it's true. Finn took over after my parents died and since most of the remaining members didn't have their parents either, I don't know. He managed to convince the others to join him in his schemes."

Vic ran a hand over the top of his head. "Wow. Okay, I'm trying to understand, so bear with me. Where are you guys from? Were you on your way somewhere when Finn pushed you out of the truck?"

Kellan rubbed a finger under his nose and nodded. "We were making our winter migration from Michigan to North Carolina. But Finn heard about a good score from a gaggle of geese that we could make on the way. I said I didn't want any part of his illegal activities anymore, refused to be their lookout, and *boom*. Out of the truck I went."

Vic was shaking his head and blinking as if in disbelief. "That's... Damn. I'm so sorry, Kellan. But at the same time, I'm glad you're no longer in those horrible circumstances. What awful shifters."

"They were real assholes. I'm glad too."

Kellan wondered if maybe Vic would take him on a tour of the town, or if he'd introduce him to his friends. He'd been serious about wanting to pay Vic back for his generosity, too. Kellan licked his lips. He would cherish any time spent with the handsome wolf.

Vic was tugging on his beard again with his brow furrowed, seemingly lost in thought. He tilted his head as he regarded Kellan. "You're going to need some clothes and toiletries. I've got plenty of toothpaste and shampoos and stuff here, but I can't think of anyone who would be about your size to borrow clothes from until we can get you some more."

Kellan hugged Vic's flannel shirt around him, crossing his arms in front of it. He didn't want Vic to take it back right away. "Sorry. The clothes I had on when I was dumped wouldn't have kept me warm enough out in the snow and I couldn't carry them around with me while shifted."

"Did you guys always leave your stuff in your vehicles when you shifted too?"

"Yeah." *I guess now Hans can have my shiny red parka he was always trying to take from me.* He'd left his jacket in the cab of the truck when they'd stopped to use the restrooms. "I was so scared, Vic. I only had my jeans, T-shirt and hoodie. Not even my boots, just my Chucks. No money, either. Finn never let me have any."

A low rumble sounded from Vic's chest then his eyes widened. "My apologies. I didn't mean for that to come out. But that brother of yours needs to be taught a lesson."

"I wish he'd get thrown in jail. All of them. They don't care *who* they steal from."

"I'm right there with you. So, you shifted. What led you this direction?"

"Well, I'm not sure exactly. I couldn't go back on the highway, it was too dangerous. It was starting to get dark and I knew I'd be in trouble if I didn't find shelter soon. Swans don't do well on their own, we always move as a group. When I went through the woods behind the rest stop, I found a small river which I thought would be perfect for me to travel on. I could make good time and I knew it would eventually lead me somewhere." Kellan smiled. "And it did."

Vic smiled back, his gorgeous hazel eyes with flecks of gold crinkling at the corners, and Kellan thought he could drown in them.

"How about I grab some more grooming stuff for you, and I can at least get you one of my T-shirts to sleep in for tonight."

Kellan supposed he could relinquish the red flannel for the tee, as long as both belonged to Vic.

Vic plucked his phone from his jean pocket. "If you give me your clothing and shoe sizes, I can pick up some stuff for you in the morning. Then, if you're up for it, I'll show you around a bit. Let you see what the place is like in the daytime."

Yes! Kellan barely stopped himself from pumping his fist in the air. "I'd love that, thank you. Do you think we could get a closer look at the lake? I'm hoping I can shift again now that I'm feeling better and I'd like to get some time in the water before it freezes over."

Vic grinned. "No worries there. The lake never freezes. You can use it year-round."

Kellan sucked in a sharp breath. *Year round?* "How come?"

"More of our town magic." Vic winked.

Kellan could barely sit still, he was so excited. The main reason swans moved around in the winter was to find water sources that weren't frozen. If he could always have the lake to float on in winter, he'd never have to go anywhere else. *I could stay here with Vic.* He gave himself a mental slap. Vic was being awfully nice, but that didn't mean the hunky wolf wanted a love-starved swan clinging to him.

"That's amazing. The whole *town* sounds amazing."

Vic nodded, still smiling. "I think so. Let me go grab those things for you."

He pushed up from the floor and when he reached his full height, Kellan was once again reminded what a large and imposing man Vic was. Kellan stared up at him with wide eyes.

So strong.

As Vic turned to leave, Kellan almost jumped from the chair to stop him. He didn't doubt that if his ankle hadn't been sprained, he would have. As if Vic had sensed his intentions, he peered over his shoulder.

"Don't worry. I won't be long."

After he'd shut the door, Kellan brought the collar of Vic's shirt to his face and pressed his nose against the fabric. He took a deep breath, closing his eyes as he remembered how comforting it had been when Vic had carried him. *Held me.*

A tear leaked from one eye at the realization that no one had touched him with any affection ever since his mom had died. It had been more than eleven years ago when he'd only been eight years old. Kellan sighed. *Don't go there. You don't need to anymore.*

He had Vale Valley and a new beginning.

CHAPTER FOUR

*V*ic tossed a small plastic bag from the drug store onto the passenger seat of his truck containing the ankle brace he'd purchased for Kellan.

Kellan.

He'd barely had any sleep. All night his mind would drift to pictures of Kellan, then he would recall his enticing scent. After jerking off two times to imaginary scenarios with Kellan moaning and writhing beneath him, he'd finally managed to drift off. He'd then spent all morning repeating the same mantra over and over in his head—the one that reminded him that big bad wolves needed to keep their hairy paws off innocent, young swans.

I'll get him settled, help him find work and introduce him to a few locals. That's it.

Vic pretended that showing Kellan around was merely him being friendly and nothing more. As the innkeeper of Vale Valley, it was his duty to be welcoming.

As he pulled into his spot in front of his cabin, he pondered where he'd like to take Kellan on their sight-seeing trip. The day was sunny, but still way below freezing. The piles of snow from the recent storm sparkled beneath the rays of the sun and made the entire town appear as magical as it truly was. He decided to play it by ear, give Kellan the highlights then let him decide.

Vic already had everything he needed for their outing. He'd brought the new clothes by earlier when they'd shared breakfast together, and he'd been relieved to discover a healthy rosy glow blooming in Kellan's cheeks when he'd arrived. After leaving Kellan so he could get ready, Vic had checked in on the inn and the restaurant. When Mark stopped by for his paycheck, he'd asked how Kellan's ankle was doing, which had then sent Vic off to get the brace.

He snatched the bag off the seat then made his way across the parking lot to the elevators. Once he'd arrived at the second floor, he headed to Kellan's room, surprised at how nervous and jumpy he was. *I saw him less than an hour ago. What the fuck.* Vic knocked on the door.

"Come in!"

He frowned then checked the knob. Sure enough, it was unlocked. Vic huffed as he entered the room.

"Why isn't the door locked? You should be more careful!"

He winced at the sight of Kellan hugging his knees to his chest and staring at him with wide eyes. His voice must have come out louder than he'd intended.

"Is it because of the dragons? I didn't think a lock could keep out any witches."

Vic rubbed his forehead. *Why did I ever tell him that?* Then again, it wasn't as if he could avoid them if he stayed in town. Vic's chest tightened. *He* has *to stay.*

"I already explained that you have nothing to fear from our dragons and witches. We're all good folk here."

"I know, I'm sorry. But Finn used to tell me horrible stories about them. After mom and dad died, he said if I didn't do everything he told me to do, he'd cut off my ears and sell me to the witches."

Vic crossed his arms as he ground his teeth. He took a couple deep breaths before responding. *No need to scare him any more than I already have.* "Finn is an asshole. You said so yourself." Vic scratched his head, trying to think of a way to make Kellan understand. "Look, I have a guy who works the front desk part-time. Mark is an initiate in the local coven and he's one of my best employees as well as a really cool person. Do you think I'd entrust my livelihood to someone if I thought they were dangerous or evil?"

Kellan lowered his head and gradually let go of his knees. "You're right. The fact that Finn was the one who told me that stuff is probably proof enough that it was all a pack of lies." He lifted his gaze. "I promise I won't embarrass you when you introduce me to your employee. I believe you." Kellan chewed his lower lip and Vic held in a groan. "I might be nervous for a while until I get to know him, but I would never be mean or rude."

Vic drew closer then sat in the other chair next to Kellan. He handed him the bag with the brace. "I know you wouldn't. I can tell you have a good heart."

They exchanged smiles and Vic sensed that another bridge had been crossed between them.

"Hey, if you're about ready, you can put on this brace then we can get going."

Kellan nodded. "I am."

He lifted up his pant leg, the jeans Vic had purchased for him a perfect fit. Vic tried to divert his pervy thoughts about how cute Kellan's ass had looked encased in them by mentally calculating how much Knight's Auto Repair was going to charge him the following week to service the transmission on his truck.

Once Kellan had finished securing the brace, he stood up and tentatively placed his weight on it.

"Is it okay?"

Kellan took a few steps. "Yeah, this is great. Thanks."

"Did you put the ice pack on it again this morning?"

He smiled. "I did."

"And your foot was elevated above your heart?"

Kellan inclined his head, a crease forming between his eyebrows. "I followed your instructions exactly, I promise. I don't lie."

Vic rubbed the back of his neck. "Right, sorry. Didn't mean to imply anything. I'm just worried, that's all."

Kellan stared at him for a moment before his lower lip began trembling. Vic rushed forward in case Kellan was in any pain and needed his help. He grabbed his upper arms.

"What's wrong?"

A tear fell from Kellan's eye. "No one's cared about what happens to me for a very long time."

Vic yanked Kellan into his embrace, cradling and rocking him. He closed his eyes, rested his head on Kellan's, losing the battle to remain indifferent to the young man. Just because he was doomed to never finding his true fated mate, it didn't mean he couldn't care about and love another. Even if in his mind it was odd that he should fall so hard and fast for Kellan, for a swan, that didn't make it *wrong*.

The way Kellan pressed his cheek to his chest and hugged him back so tightly was nothing short of a confirmation that he was feeling the same way. He still intended to try and slow things down, if only to allow poor Kellan the chance to adjust to his new world, along with discovering his place within it.

Kellan loosened his hold and gazed up at Vic. "Is it okay that I like you and think you're very handsome?"

Yup. That's a rather direct confirmation. "Only if it's okay that I like you and think you're very beautiful."

Kellan grinned. "Really? You think I'm beautiful? Finn always said—"

Vic placed a finger against Kellan's lips. "Hey, let's forget about him for now. I realize it's going to take you a long time before for you to heal from what he and the rest of the herd did to you, but for now, maybe you can practice telling yourself that he was a horrible person who only wanted to hurt you, that none of what he said was true. What do you think?" Vic rubbed his thumb across Kellan's soft cheek.

"I think you're right, about everything." He sighed. "You know, I still can't believe that any of this is real. I never thought I'd find somewhere safe or someone who cared about me at all, let alone..." Kellan ducked his head.

"Hey." Vic placed a knuckle beneath Kellan's chin and encouraged him to look up. "You don't have to hide from me. Ever. Now, you were going to say?"

Kellan's brow wrinkled. "I don't want you to think I'm pushy."

Vic gave him a half-smile. He had an idea what Kellan might be driving at. After all, he'd spent all night and half the morning trying to tell himself he wasn't falling for a near-stranger.

"I've been worried you'll think *I'm* pushy. Tell me."

Kellan cleared his throat. "I was going to say, let alone that I might find a mate."

Vic's heart swelled, and in that moment, he knew his feelings weren't simply a case of misplaced lust, that Kellan meant something to him, that he had been led to Vale Valley for more than sanctuary. They might not be able to have a family since they couldn't possibly be fated mates, but that was all right. They'd still have each other.

"Kellan, have you ever been kissed?"

Kellan blinked up at him as he shook his head.

Vic framed Kellan's face with his hands. "Then I think we should do something about that."

He held Kellan's gaze for a moment before descending on him, capturing Kellan's lips with his own, moving them over Kellan's mouth. He kept his touch slow and gentle, imprinting the memory of their first kiss to hold dear in his heart forever. Kellan melted against his frame and kissed him back, his technique clumsy, but earnest. As their exchange heated, Vic wrapped one hand around Kellan's nape and grasped his waist with the other. Kellan opened up to him and Vic dipped his tongue into Kellan's willing mouth, tasting and exploring as much of the sweet man as he could.

Vic slowed the kiss before they got too carried away, still mindful of not overwhelming him. When he broke the connection, he framed Kellan's face again and pressed his lips to Kellan's forehead to seal his intent. They stared into each other's eyes in silence as they caught their breath again.

Kellan curled his fingers in the fabric of Vic's flannel shirt, clutching it as if he were scared Vic might run away. "That was... I don't know how to describe it. Why do you taste so good?" He shivered. "I feel strange, like I'm about to burst out of my skin."

Vic rubbed Kellan's back, trying to soothe him. "You've been through so much in the past twenty-four hours and you've just been kissed for the first time." Vic smiled. "You're bound to feel on edge."

The confusion in Kellan's expression remained. *Yes. Definitely have to slow things down.* "Why don't we go enjoy ourselves, see the sights? I have the whole afternoon free. When we come back, I'll introduce you to the restaurant staff. When your ankle gets better, you're welcome to help out there. Or, I can introduce you to some other people if there's something else you'd rather do."

"Oh no, I'll help at the restaurant. I don't want to be

anywhere but here." His cheeks flushed. "If that's okay with you."

Vic broke into a grin. "More than okay." He let go of Kellan and plucked the jacket he'd bought Kellan that morning off the bed then held it out to him. "Ready to see your new home?"

Kellan grinned back. "Yes." He sighed. "My new home."

Vic helped him with the jacket and made a silent vow that he'd do everything in his power to keep Kellan safe and happy from then on. The young swan wasn't the only one who never thought they'd find someone who cared that much about them.

~

*K*ellan kept twisting and turning his head, trying to see all the sights of the downtown at once. The town was small—Vic had told him that at last count it held about five thousand residents. Apparently, the town was also protected through the magic of a witch who recently died, but her sister— Rosemary Vale, the town's mayor and a werewolf—was the current keeper of the magic.

Kellan was becoming more and more amazed at the various aspects that made up Vale Valley. He'd never known such a place existed, or that it was even a possibility. But now that he did, he never wanted to leave. He snuck a sideways glance at Vic. *Did he mean what he said? That he wants me too?*

Kellan tried to sit still, tried not to squirm in his seat so much, but he couldn't stop. He hadn't been exaggerating earlier when he'd told Vic he was about to jump out of his skin. *Maybe it's that witch magic.* Whatever he was going through might not be evil, but it sure as hell was potent.

"Oh, look. They're hanging their sign." Vic pointed to a pretty shop on the right side of the street. "That's Sweet Bites. It's a new creperie opening up next week." Vic squeezed Kellan's hand before returning it to the wheel. "We should give them a try."

Kellan bounced twice before he realized what he was doing and immediately made himself stop. The urge to start up again was *huge*, but he'd do his best not to. "I'd love that. I've never had a crepe before."

"Then I'll put it at the top of our list."

Our. It was a great word. "Can we go to the lake before it's time to head back to the restaurant?"

"Of course we can."

"Ooh, what's that?" Kellan pointed to a modern, two story building next to a small market.

"Oh, that's my friend Grayson's Creatures of Comfort aromatherapy shop and health center. I do my work outs there." Vic pulled into an open parking space in the small lot. "Grayson is one of the Vales. Rosemary is his grandmother."

Something about the shop intrigued Kellan. He pressed his nose against the window of the truck. "Wow. Does everyone here know each other?"

Vic chuckled. "Seems that way, doesn't it? No, we don't, but we *do* have each other's backs."

"What's aromatherapy?" He couldn't take his eyes off the place.

"Um, I'm not sure I'm the best person to explain this, but people use different scented oils and combinations of oils to help boost their emotions and..."

When Vic didn't continue, Kellan looked over his shoulder to see why. He was met with Vic's deep frown as he rubbed his bearded chin.

"What else does it help with, Vic?"

"Like I said, not my thing. My nose is so sensitive, I usually avoid that part of the center. If you want, we can go inside and check it out."

"Can we? Thanks, Vic. It looks amazing."

Vic helped him down from the truck and they entered the large establishment. Everything was bright and sleek with an open floor plan. A fireplace was on one side and the second story was where all the gym equipment was. Apparently, rooms were available for massages as well, but what really interested Kellan was the elegant aromatherapy shop in the center of the first floor. Vic gathered up his hand and led him toward it.

A pretty young woman glanced up from behind one of the display cases. "Hello, gentlemen, what can I help you with today?"

Kellan didn't know how to respond since he didn't understand about the aromatherapy. Vic spoke up and took Kellan off the hook.

"Hi Flora. I've been trying to explain to my friend Kellan here what this aromatherapy business is all about."

Flora laughed. "That's okay, Vic. I gotcha covered." She beckoned Kellan over. "It's nice to meet you, Kellan."

She's very friendly. "It's nice to meet you, too."

Flora tapped a finger against her lip. "Let me see. Is there anything that's been bothering you lately, something you wish you had some help with?"

If she'd asked him the same question the day before, his answers would've been a lot different. "Well, I had a big scare yesterday, but everything's much better now."

"Oh, I see. I'm sorry about yesterday, but I'm glad things are looking up today." She reached into a case and pulled out several tiny vials. "I want you to sniff each of these, and tell me whether you're drawn to them or not."

Kellan sniffed and picked out a few of the scents that he enjoyed the best, then he watched in fascination as Flora mixed then together in a new bottle. Eventually, they walked out of the shop with a mixture for calming his nerves and a bath bomb for relaxation. Vic had appeared skeptical, however, he'd insisted on purchasing the items for him.

When they got back to the truck again, Kellan clutched the gift from Vic, holding the bag tightly and trying not to get emotional again. Vic was going to think he was weak or goofy in the head, and that's not what he was like at all. He'd had to be resilient in order to survive the daily bashings he'd endured at the hands of Finn, as well as the other herd members when they were trying to kiss up to his rotten brother.

"Okay, next stop, the lake." Vic regarded him before putting the truck in reverse. "You must be hungry. I know my stomach's getting a bit growly."

Kellan imagined Vic had a big appetite. *All those muscles.* He bit his lip to temper his arousal. Being held by Vic earlier had been amazing. He'd wanted to climb the man like a tree.

"Whatever you want, Vic. If you're hungry, then we should eat."

He smiled. "You're a sweetheart. How about this? We'll head back to the restaurant and grab a bite, I'll show you around there, then we can go to the lake at sunset. Sound good?"

Kellan sighed. "Sounds romantic."

Vic's eyes widened a bit and he cleared his throat. "Is that okay?" He pulled out of the space then headed in the direction of the inn.

"It is for me."

The corner of Vic's mouth turned up in a smile. "Cool. To the restaurant we go, then lake at sunset."

Kellan sat back in his seat, still cradling the gift Vic had bought him and trying to relax. *Best day ever.* He wiggled and clenched his fists. *If only I could get rid of this jumpiness.*

CHAPTER FIVE

*V*ic leaned against the walk-in cooler in the restaurant kitchen, going over the bar list to verify the liquor order. The upcoming holidays meant an increase in sales for certain items.

Champagne. He always carried a few bottles of premium then several mid-range brands. *Brandy, rum, bourbon, top shelf scotch...* Vic plucked at his beard as he pondered whether to add to his coffee liqueur order from the previous year. By the time New Year's Eve had rolled around, he'd run out of a few.

"Hiya boss man."

Vic glanced up from his clipboard to see his head cook, Skip, ambling in from the back door for his dinner shift. "Hey, Skip." He set the clipboard down on the prep table stool. "Have our turkeys come in yet?"

"Nope. Only the hams."

"The sweet potatoes?"

"Yup. Two crates full." Skip moved around the kitchen, taking tops off of sauce pans in the warmer, stirring the soup of the day and getting his pans out. "Did Chester finish washing the skillets from lunch service?"

Vic crossed his arms. "Skip? Can you focus for a second?"

The older wolf, a beta from what was left of Vic's pack, turned to face him while scratching his apron-covered round belly. "Yeah?"

Vic kept his eye-roll to himself. "Chester is on break and I'm sure he'll be happy to share that with you when he gets back. I haven't been here most of the afternoon. But I was—"

"Problems at the inn?"

Vic let out an aggravated sigh. "No. Personal business. As I was saying—"

"What kind of personal business?"

He pinched the bridge of his nose. It was a damn good thing everything was different now that they were in Vale. He might be Alpha, but he'd let a lot of the old pack dynamics go once their rag-tag bunch had arrived. *I'm still his damn boss, though.*

"*Skip.* It's personal and it's none of your business. May I continue?"

Skip harrumphed and mumbled under his breath. "I ain't stopping you."

"I'd like to order a third crate of sweet potatoes. And those garnet yams."

Skip arched his eyebrows. "That's a sweet potato."

Vic frowned. "But... Well, how do you tell the difference between them?"

"The sweet potato is the one that tastes good and the yam is the one that tastes like shit."

Goddess help me. "Okay, how about this. However you can manage it, I'd like to make sure you have at least three crates of the ones that taste good and..." *Kellan seems to like a lot of vegetables.* "How about one crate of the shitty ones, just in case."

Skip shook his head and snorted. "Whatever you say, boss. It's your dog and pony show."

Vic didn't even want to ask. "Thanks. Also, keep an eye on the turkey situation. A lot of people in town and the whole staff rely on us having dinner for them here on Thanksgiving, and I don't want anyone disappointed."

Skip gave him a thumbs up then went about his work. After doing his best to keep his concentration on the alcohol order, instead of on getting back to Kellan, Vic decided it looked good and hung the clipboard on the peg for the bar manager to take care of in the morning. All he wanted was to join Kellan who was waiting for him in the dining room.

The moment Vic spotted him sitting in one of the booths near the host station, his heart picked up a quicker pace. The dinner crowd wouldn't start coming in for another hour or so, and only one person sat at the counter that was in front of the open kitchen, two guys at the bar on one side of the dining room, and a young couple in a corner booth. The restaurant famous for it's American-style comfort eats was edged with booths on two sides, the bar and counter on the others. Like the inn, the primary color scheme incorporated green, although Vic had made a concession by letting Dora have a red carnation in a bud vase at each table. Once twilight hit, then the small brass and crystal candle lamps would be lit.

As he drew closer to the booth, he could detect Kellan's scent, which he could swear was even more pungent than the day before. *Maybe it's that I'm anticipating it.* Kellan glanced up when he was almost at the table.

Kellan gave him a wide grin. "Everything okay in the kitchen?"

Vic slid into the booth next to Kellan and draped his arm over the top of the banquette. "Fine. I hope you haven't been too bored?"

"Not at all. I've been memorizing the menu for when I start working and Dora told me the table numbers. Do you want to quiz me?"

Vic imagined he was smiling like a loon. Something about Kellan filled him with such happiness. In some ways, it was if he'd been awoken from a deep sleep, as if he'd been merely existing all these years, trudging along without any purpose, and was somehow alive again.

He played with the ends of Kellan's hair, lightly tugging at the platinum strands that kissed the top of his collar. "That's all right, I'm sure you'll do great. You and Dora are getting along good, then?"

"She's nice." Kellan glanced over his shoulder, glancing toward the kitchen. He leaned closer to Vic and spoke next to his ear. "She said to watch out for Skip, that's he's a grump."

Vic chuckled. "That he is. He's harmless, but if he's rude to you, let me know. Sometimes he gets a bit too mouthy."

While Vic was sure Kellan could handle himself, he also worried about how much he'd been talked down to by Finn for most of his young life. He didn't need to be treated poorly in his new home, too.

"I will, Vic."

"Say, do you like yams?"

"Sure. I like all vegetables and most fruits. I don't care for grapefruit too much." Kellan scrunched his forehead. "Why?"

Vic gave a one-shouldered shrug. "I was doing the ordering for Thanksgiving. Plus, I think I should learn more about what you like and don't like, don't you think?"

Kellan grinned. "I want to do the same with you. What's your favorite thing to eat on Thanksgiving?"

"Oh, that's easy. The turkey." Vic gasped. "Wait. You said you had geese for cousins. Are turkeys...?"

Kellan giggle-snorted. "No, we're not related. However, I don't eat any bird, so don't be offended if I don't have any turkey."

"Don't worry about that. Eat whatever you want." Vic trailed his fingers over Kellan's shoulder, unable to keep from constantly touching him. "We'll have ham too."

"I'm afraid I only eat fish or other water creatures."

Vic considered that. He didn't want Kellan to feel left out. "I could have Skip fix you something special for that day."

Kellan grabbed his arm. "Oh no, don't do that. The yams sound great and I love cranberries and potatoes. If I have that and pumpkin pie, I'll barely be able to move as it is, I'll be so stuffed."

Vic took Kellan's hand and laced their fingers together. "I'll make sure you have plenty."

"Well hello, dear. I got your message."

Vic turned his head at the sound of Rosemary Vale's voice from behind him. He let go of Kellan and slid out of the booth to greet her.

"Hello, ma'am. Thank you for stopping by. You didn't have to go to all that trouble, though. We could've spoken on the phone."

The attractive, dark-haired older woman laughed. "Would I have been able to get a piece of your splendid apple pie over the phone?" She whacked the air with her hand. "I don't think so." She gazed down at Kellan and a smile tugged at her lips. "May I join you both?"

"Yes, of course, please." He gestured for her to go ahead.

Vic waited until she took the seat opposite them in the booth then sat down again. He got the attention of the server, John.

"Rosemary, would you like some coffee with your pie?"

Her eyes crinkled as she smiled. "That would be wonderful." She addressed John. "Do you mind putting that in a to-go container? I'll have a bite here then take the rest with me to save for later."

John nodded then left to get her order. Vic regarded Rosemary.

"Rosemary, this is the swan shifter I was telling you about in my message, Kellan... er..." He turned to Kellan. "What's your last name?"

"Rivers."

Vic nodded then returned his attention to Rosemary. He was about to speak when it hit him what Kellan had said. "Rivers? For real?"

"Sure. My mother's maiden name was Waters."

"Huh. Cool." He regarded Rosemary again. "As I was saying, this is Kellan Rivers."

Rosemary let out a light laugh. "Very nice to meet you Kellan Rivers. I imagine you know who I am by now, but I'll formally introduce myself so we get off on the right foot, so to speak. I'm Rosemary Vale."

She extended her hand across the table and Kellan took it. Her head tilted, and her eyes narrowed a fraction as she wrapped her fingers around his. A flash of something passed over her features and she darted her gaze at Vic before returning it to Kellan. She gave Kellan's hand a solid shake then let go. Kellan smiled back at her and Vic could tell he was at ease with the town's mayor.

John brought her the coffee and pie, along with Vic's iced tea that he couldn't get enough of, even when it was freezing outside. So far, all Kellan wanted to drink was lots of water, so Vic had made sure he had plenty of it.

Rosemary popped open the waxed cardboard flaps of the to-go container. She cut off a forkful of the pie and rolled her eyes back in her head as she chewed. "Oh goodness. Magnificent, as always." She set down the utensil then closed up the box. "Now tell me, Kellan. Will we have the pleasure of your company here in Vale Valley for a long time, I hope?"

"Can I stay, then? I really want to."

Rosemary chuckled then patted Kellan's hand. "You don't need my permission for that. If you want to be a member of the town, I'll add you on our list. But the very fact that you found us means you're supposed to be here. Ultimately, though, the choice is yours whether you'll stay."

Vic noted with amusement that Kellan bounced on the seat a couple times.

"Then yes, I'll *definitely* stay." He gazed up at Vic. "I've never been treated so well."

Vic took Kellan's hand again and gave it a squeeze. "You deserve the best."

"My, my." Rosemary smiled at them over her coffee cup. "This is good. Very good." She took a sip then set it down. "I'm afraid Vic has allowed past tragedies and getting lost in work keep him from allowing anyone near his heart." She took another drink. "But that's probably for the best. Good things come to those who wait." Rosemary chuckled again. "Or perhaps I should say, the *right* things."

Kellan had been staring at her very intently as she spoke. "Can I ask you a question, ma'am? Because you seem like you know about a lot of things."

"Of course, dear. I'll do the best I can. What did you want to know?"

"Well..." Kellan wrapped his hands around his water glass as he drew his eyebrows together. "I haven't been able to shift since I was out lost in the woods. And actually, at one point, I couldn't stay shifted either. It would last for a few minutes, then poof! I'd go back to human again. I thought maybe after I'd warmed up and had some rest, I'd be fine." His lip trembled slightly. "Do you think I'm broken?"

Rosemary reached across the table and patted his arm. "How old are you, Kellan?"

Kellan straightened in his seat and Vic frowned. *What's that got to do with anything?*

"I just turned nineteen."

She nodded sagely. "I see. And in your herd, were you an egg-layer?"

He shrugged. "Well, yeah. But I've never laid any before. There weren't any mated pairs in our herd, so our roles weren't defined very well. It was more about Finn telling everyone what to do."

Vic hadn't thought to ask about mates or anything such as that. Kellan's herd had clearly been a rogue faction of swans.

Rosemary took a hearty swallow of her coffee and seemed to drain the cup. "That's very unusual for a group of swans to be unmated like that. They must have gotten into a lot of trouble because of it." She shook her head. "I'm so glad you were able to get away from them, Kellan." She patted his arm again, then gathered up her coat that she'd lain on the seat beside her. "I wouldn't worry, Kellan. It will all work itself out in time."

Kellan shoulders relaxed and he smiled. "Okay, thank you."

Vic pressed his lips in a thin line. He didn't want to get bitchy with Rosemary in front of Kellan, but *his* concerns about Kellan hadn't been answered. Not being able to shift sounded very serious to him.

As Rosemary got to her feet, Vic jumped up to help her with her coat.

"Kellan? I'll be right back. I'd like to walk Mrs. Vale to her car."

"Sure, Vic. I know I'm too young to serve it yet, but I'll learn the wine list too."

Once they were out of Kellan's hearing range, Vic spoke. "I don't mean to criticize you, but how can you know everything will sort itself out with Kellan regarding his ability to shift? Don't you think we should call in a shifting expert?"

They reached her car and she stopped and turned to face him. "I can already tell how much you care about him, and it's clear he adores you too."

He hadn't realized how obvious it was to those around them. "Um, yeah. But I'm not sure how that relates to his inability to shift?"

Rosemary gave him a knowing smile. "Swans can't shift when they go into heat." She patted his arm, much the same as she'd done to Kellan. "Once he's been mated, he'll be fine."

Vic's jaw went slack. "Whoa, wait, hold up. Male swans can lay eggs?"

Rosemary pursed her lips then shook her head. "Vic, my dear, you've been living in your own world for much too long. You reside in a town where the entire male population—shifters, elemental spirits and humans alike—can have a child, and you find it surprising that a male swan can lay eggs?"

"I..." He ran a hand over the top of his head. "Yeah, I guess that sounded kind of dumb. But, it's not as if I can impregnate... or, how would that work? I mean, I'm a wolf."

"Yes, dear, you are." Rosemary grabbed both of his biceps and gave him a shake. She might be older than dirt, but she'd always been a strong Alpha wolf and that hadn't dulled with age. "Why don't you let nature and the fates take its course, hmm?" She released him then opened the door to her car. "Now, if you'll excuse me, I'm having the family over tonight."

The smile she gave him held a lot of mystery and Vic wished he could convince her to reveal more about Kellan and the mating rituals of swans.

"Thanks, ma'am. Can I call you if I have any more questions?"

Rosemary climbed into the driver's seat and gazed up at him. "Call anytime, ask what you want. Answers?" She grinned. "Maybe." Rosemary barked out a laugh then shut the door.

As Vic watched her drive away, he blew into his hands again, the sharp blast of cold reminding him that he needed to verify that Kellan was bundled up well before they went to view the sunset at the lake.

Heat?

He supposed she was right, why couldn't a male swan or any other avian shifter lay eggs? Vic glanced back at the restaurant where Kellan sat waiting for his return. Everything inside him screamed that Kellan was meant to be with him—had been drawn to Vale Valley so they could be together—but he hadn't considered that they could be *fated* mates.

Maybe I have been wallowing in my loneliness for much too long.

CHAPTER SIX

*K*ellan had finally convinced Vic that his ankle was fine and that he could start working in the restaurant. While he sat on the edge of the bed and adjusted the brace to give him some extra support, his thoughts drifted to a couple nights before when he and Vic had sat on a bench at sunset, arm and arm, with Kellan resting his head on Vic's shoulder. His protective wolf had taken the wool blanket—that had kept Kellan warm the night Vic had rescued him—then laid it on the bench so he wouldn't get as chilly. After it had gotten too cold to stay any longer, they had walked hand in hand back to the restaurant for some apple pie and hot cocoa.

He sighed. *I like him so much.*

It was silly how much he'd missed Vic the day before when he'd had to go to a town almost two hours away to pick up some supplies for the restaurant. Kellan appreciated how involved Vic was with his business, was impressed by his work ethic. He'd missed him like crazy, though. His day had been spent hanging out at the restaurant, reading a well-used copy of A Christmas Carol in the lobby by the fireplace, taking a nice warm bath with

his new oils and trying not to count the minutes until Vic
returned.

Kellan grabbed his coat. Even though he'd only be outside in
the cold for a few minutes, from the way Vic fussed over and
worried about him, he knew he'd be in trouble if he didn't have it
on. A sly smile tugged at his lips as he remembered the rather
long bath he'd taken. He'd never masturbated all that much—zero
privacy—but he'd been bizarrely horny from almost the moment
he'd seen Vic.

As he stepped off the elevator that landed him in the lobby
right behind reception, he noticed that Mark was there. He froze
right outside the elevator doors and was about to dart back
through them when they abruptly slid shut. His mouth went dry
and he couldn't make himself move.

He's a good guy. Vic likes him.

Mark certainly *seemed* okay. Not evil at all.

I can't be late my first day.

He sucked in a deep breath and made a run for it when Mark
appeared absorbed in something on the computer. As he breezed
past, he threw a greeting over his shoulder.

"Good afternoon, Mark!"

Half of Mark's response was lost as Kellan scurried down the
short hall to the restaurant, the doors to the entrance closing and
cutting off Mark's final words. Kellan stopped and caught his
breath, tugging off the coat that had now become stifling. Vic kept
his place nice and cozy.

Dora waved at him from behind the cash register. "Hi, hon.
Ready for your big day?"

Kellan hung his jacket on an arm of the bentwood coatrack in
the corner of the small waiting area. "I think so. I studied the
menu again last night and I'll run over the table numbers with
you again. Any specials for tonight?"

Vic had been in town all morning but would be stopping in to join him for dinner. It was two o'clock, the lunch rush was over, and it had been decided the day before that between the meal services would be a good time for him to get up to speed. Few people came in the middle of the afternoon, usually just coffee drinkers with their laptops or the older residents taking their dinner early.

Dora had been busy shuffling through some notes. "Darn it." She tapped her fingers on the counter and let out a long sigh. "The host on the early shift didn't leave anything about the specials, not even today's soup. I should've double-checked."

"That's okay, Dora. I'll go ask Skip for you. Do have a pen and piece of paper? I'll write it down."

"Aww, thanks. That would be awesome."

Right as she handed him the items he'd requested, the outside restaurant door opened. The brass bell above the threshold jangled and a burst of cold air blew in. The young couple who stepped inside began removing their stocking hats and gloves and shaking some of the tiny flakes of snow from their hair. Dora grabbed a couple menus and led them to a booth on the other end that would place them far from the cold air that would whoosh in every time someone entered the restaurant.

My first customers. Kellan's heart thundered. *I can do this.* If he could handle being treated like garbage by his brother, waiting on friendly people should be no problem. While he was sure there would be the occasional cranky customer, so far everyone he'd met had seemed happy and content. *As if they're living in a fairy tale.*

Kellan grinned as he made his way to the back. *Finn and the rest of those jerks can be miserable and unhappy. Not me. Not anymore.*

When he reached the swinging door that led to the kitchen, he nudged it with his shoulder and pushed his way through.

"Hi Skip, I'm here for my first day."

He grabbed the apron that Vic had left for him off a hook and tucked an empty checkbook into one of the pockets. He'd find out what the specials were then bring the list back to Dora. *I can memorize it on the way.* There were plenty of pens to be had in a round, metal holder next to the checkbook stacks, so he grabbed a couple of those as well.

Skip was muttering from where he stood on the line, lifting metal lids off various food containers, stirring a few things here and there with the long-handled stainless-steel scoops, then replacing the coverings. He hadn't acknowledged Kellan's greeting yet, so he figured Skip mustn't have heard him.

Kellan raised his voice a bit louder. "Good afternoon, Skip. I'm here for my first day."

Skip banged down the cover he'd been holding then whipped his head around, glaring at Kellan. "I can *see* that. I'm not an idiot, you know. Quit bothering me, I've got stuff to take care of and you're in the way." He returned to what he'd been doing, showing Kellan his back.

Kellan twisted his hands and, in the process, mangled the paper Dora had given him. His stomach clenched, his legs shaking as he agonized over his next move. He had customers, they'd want to know what the soup was for the day, what specials there were. He'd also promised Dora he'd find out what they were, so she wouldn't have to.

"Gods, you are so useless, Kellan." Finn's favorite insult toward him came to life in his mind. *"You're not like the rest of us. Not smart. Not strong. How dare you try and act like you are?"* Sometimes, if Finn lost his temper too badly, he'd smack him across the face. Kellan's hand went to his cheek, and without thinking, he ran from the kitchen.

By the time he'd made it back to the front, he saw that Dora must have taken the couples' drink order. The host did that most of the time anyway, but Kellan felt as if he'd already failed. He reached the front register where she stood busily restocking the gum and mint stand on the counter. His shoulders slumped and he lowered his head, ashamed that he hadn't been able to handle something so simple.

Finn's been right this whole time. I don't know what I was thinking.

"Hey, what's wrong?"

He glanced up to see Dora's worried expression. Her brow wrinkled as her gaze traveled to the mangled piece of paper she'd given him which he still held clutched between his fingers.

"I'm sorry, Dora. I didn't find out what the specials are or anything."

She pinched her lips together and placed her hands on her hips, her frown deepening. *Now she'll be mad at me too and tell Vic that I'm hopeless at this job.* He didn't know what he'd do if Vic was angry and disappointed with him.

"Did Skip mouth off at you?" She let out a small growl which reminded Kellan that Vic had told him she was a bobcat shifter. "I'll claw his eyes out!"

Kellan blinked repeatedly as it sunk in that she wasn't mad at him, but at Skip. "I didn't mean to get anyone in trouble."

She snorted. "He makes plenty of his own trouble. He's a sour old wolf who should be taught a lesson."

Kellan's stomach clenched again. Whenever Finn would say that to him, it would be awful. He didn't want to be responsible for anyone getting hurt, no matter how rude they were.

"Please don't do that." He chewed on his lip as he shredded the last bits of the poor piece of paper. "Maybe... maybe he's calmed down now. I'll go try again."

Dora crossed her arms. "Are you sure? I can tell he upset you."

He nodded his head before he could change his mind and shake it. "Can I have another piece of paper?"

She sighed then tore him off a sheet from a small spiral note-book. "I hope you guys straighten this out before Vic gets here, otherwise I'm betting he'll go all Alpha on Skip's ass since it's clear he's taken you under his protection."

Kellan's eyes widened. "I'd better hurry then." He glanced over his shoulder as he remembered his customers. Their menus were closed and had been pushed to the edge of the table. "Oh no, they're ready to order."

Dora came out from behind the register. "Let me at least grab this for you, hon."

He regarded her. "Okay, thanks." Kellan smiled, his nerves finally calming a bit. "We'll share."

While Dora took the customers' orders, Kellan headed back to the kitchen to face his nemesis. He wasn't sure if pretending nothing had happened was the best move—that strategy had never worked out well for him with Finn—or if he should attempt to start over with the surly cook.

When he reached the swinging door, he peeked through the round safety window. At first, he couldn't spot Skip, but then he popped out from behind the rack of pies. Kellan jumped, even though Skip had no idea he was there spying on him. He inhaled deeply and tugged on the bottom of his apron before pushing his way into the kitchen again.

"Skip? We need to know what tonight's specials and the soup of the day are." He held his breath as he braced himself for the explosion.

Skip rubbed his chin then held up a finger. "Lemme check the walk-in real quick."

Kellan let out in a rush the big breath he'd been holding. He frowned, surprised at Skip's sudden change of attitude. Skip reappeared a minute later.

"Let's see, today's the last day for that walleye, so I'll do it pan-fried with an herbed crust. Choice of baked potato or sweet potato fries on the side, and the veggie is green beans with almonds. Make it fourteen ninety-five. I also have six orders of the pork chops from yesterday too. Same price on that."

Kellan scribbled everything down as Skip described, then took a chance by offering a comment and a smile. "Sounds good."

Skip jerked up his head and regarded Kellan. He grunted. "Yeah, well, I've been doing this for a while." He checked under one of the lids on the line. "Looks like Dan made up a big batch of chicken noodle soup this morning." After covering it again, he stuck his thumbs in the bib of his apron. "So, uh, sorry about earlier. You seem like a nice kid. I've just got a headache, that's all."

Kellan arched his eyebrows. "Apology accepted." He cleared his throat as he called every ounce of his nerve to the surface. "But I'd appreciate it if you wouldn't yell at me and I promise not to yell at you, either." He swallowed hard as he waited for Skip's reaction.

Skip pursed his lips as he rocked on his heels. Finally, he let out another grunt. "Deal. Don't like being snarled at either."

Kellan broke into a wide smile. "Awesome. Um, I guess I'd better get out there so I don't leave Dora alone."

Right as he was pushing through the door, Skip called out, "Hey, kid. I'll save a piece of the fish for you."

Kellan gave Skip a quick nod in acknowledgement. "Thanks, Skip. That's really nice of you."

As he made his way through the dining room to share with Dora what specials they had, his heart was much lighter and not only was he no longer intimidated by the grouchy cook, but he thought he might grow to like him after a while. For all he knew, Skip was all alone or maybe he'd lost his mate when the virus killed off Vic's pack members. Kellan decided he'd ask Vic about it later.

But one truth remained above everything else. At the same

time the previous week, he'd been miserable and unhappy with his brother and their rag-tag, outlaw herd of swans. His future had seemed bleak and he'd felt trapped and alone. If Vic finding him wasn't destined, then the way he saw it, no such thing as destiny existed at all.

*V*ic had found a supplier a couple of towns over who had an amazing crop of fresh, organic cranberries, and he'd managed to score the last two pallets of them. Skip would undoubtedly grouse and stomp around, barking at him that they were going to be stuck with a whole pallet of the non-organic ones. Of course, Vic had taken that into consideration already, but he'd let Skip bellyache about it for a while to get it out of his system.

Every year, the winter holidays in Vale Valley were magnificent, the entire town going all out when it came to decorations and celebrating. Vic loved the holidays too, always had. But after losing his folks, brother and two sisters to the virus—his heart would grow heavy right around the beginning of November and remain that way through New Year's. The memories of being with his family at Thanksgiving and Christmas were both beautiful and agonizing. The bitter reality of having lost them and the certainty that he'd never find a mate had made it a challenge to participate as enthusiastically in the festivities as he would've liked.

That's all changed now.

Vic hoisted the first pallet of berries from the bed of his truck and trudged to the back entrance of the restaurant. His first order of business when he got inside, and after Skip was done complaining, would be to find Kellan and steal a kiss. Then, he planned on sitting with Kellan in one of the back booths with a few baskets of cranberries, a spool of thread and a couple of needles. They were going to string up their own decorations, make it into something fun they could share every year.

Like we did when I was growing up.

Maybe it wasn't quite time for Christmas decorations yet, but they could also take some mini pumpkins, acorn squash and fancy gourds and group them together to make lovely centerpieces for the upcoming Thanksgiving feast.

Then, we can string the cranberries. He rubbed his chin. *They might go bad before Christmas.* Vic shrugged to himself. *Oh well, we can string more.* He smiled. *And some popcorn, too.*

Vic whistled *Winter Wonderland* as he finished bringing the second pallet in and adding it on top of the first. He plucked off his work gloves then shoved them into the pockets of his Sherpa-lined nylon jacket. The down parka had been retired until further notice. Skip appeared from around the corner, wiping his hands on a towel.

"Hiya, boss. What are those cranberries for? We already got some."

Vic hung his jacket on top of Kellan's. He wished Skip had given him another sixty seconds alone in the back before materializing. He'd hoped to get a hearty whiff of Kellan's scent from his coat after missing him so much all day. Of course, he'd have the real thing in a bit, but he didn't think it was appropriate to be huffing Kellan's neck out in the dining room of his restaurant during dinner service.

"Hey, Skip." He pointed to the new pallets. "Have your prep guy make a place in the walk-in for these. They're organic, so let's use them for the sauce and the glaze on the..." Vic slapped a hand to his mouth. "Oh shit."

Skip narrowed his eyes as he examined the new berries as if they were somehow defective. "Something wrong?"

"Is it too late to cancel the duck order?"

Skip straightened with a frown. "Cancel? Are you crazy or something? The locals will have your hide. You know, a couple people inquired whether we were going to have goose this year as well, like you once promised. I said I'd talk to—"

"Oh, no. No, no, no." Vic frantically waved his arms around.

Skip frowned. "What's the matter with you? This job finally sending you over the edge?"

"Dammit, Skip. Kellan is a *swan* shifter."

He shrugged. "So? We're not serving any swan. Plus, he eats chicken, don't he? Everyone eats chicken."

Vic pinched the bridge of his nose and sighed. "No, Skip. Not *everyone* eats chicken. *He* doesn't. And ducks and geese are related to swans, they're in the same family or something, I dunno. But what I *do* know is that I'll be donating my down parka to Rafe's homeless shelter and if it's too late to cancel the duck order, then they'll be getting those too."

Skip scratched his head. "I'm confused. Are we keeping the turkeys you already ordered for them then giving them the ducks instead?"

Vic scrubbed his face with both hands. *I need a drink.* "No. They can have both. Look, no ducks, no geese. People can eat turkey or ham."

"For Christmas too? Everyone wants duck or goose at Christmas."

Vic let out a low growl. "One major feast at a time, Skip, okay?"

Skip rolled his eyes and shook his head. "Sure, boss man. Whatever you say."

"Good. I'm gonna go check on the front. Did you sell the rest of the pork chops yet?"

"Nah, I have two orders left. Want one?"

"Yeah, that sounds great. Couple baked potatoes, too. I'm

starving, it's been a long day." Vic tried to recall what else they had that Kellan might like.

"Oh, hey. I saved a piece of walleye for swan boy."

Vic held in a retort. "That'll be fine, Skip. Thanks. I'll see if he can take his break."

Skip snorted. "I'm sure it won't be a problem. Been dead out there again today."

He nodded. It wasn't unusual for the time of year, but he still hated when it got too slow. *At least I can sit with my...* Vic swallowed hard, his heart fluttering as he let the truth sink in of what being with Kellan meant. He could fight the compulsion raging through him all he wanted. The urge to protect and care for the beautiful Kellan might not make any sense, but it was undeniable. How could a wolf mate with a swan? He might not understand why fate had chosen them to be together, yet one thing was now clear to him—he would never let Kellan go.

Does he feel the same?

If it was too soon for Kellan, if he was still hurting from what his herd had done to him, Vic wouldn't push. Kellan was young. When he was ready to be mated, he would let Vic know.

Rosemary doesn't know Kellan's whole story. The town's mayor likely assumed it was the onset of Kellan's heat that was preventing him from shifting instead of the fact that he'd been traumatized and injured. They could worry about heats, mating and all that other stuff later. And anyway, a half-swan, half wolf baby? Didn't make any sense. Kellan might never carry any children for them, which was fine too. A thread of melancholy coursed through him at the thought, but he was so happy to have Kellan, he didn't dare question fate any more than he had already.

The moment he spotted Kellan up at the register with Dora, seemingly lost in thought as he chewed on the end of his pen while pointing at something on the counter, he broke into a grin.

Vic had always been quiet and would keep to himself, so he was sure his staff was more than aware of how smitten he was with Kellan. It was impossible to hide.

Kellan caught his gaze and smiled, his features brightening. He set down the pen as he said something to Dora then came rushing over. He threw his arms around Vic's neck and Vic embraced him back.

"You're here! I hope you've been having a good day."

He turned up his chin and Vic got the hint. Vic captured his mouth in a soft kiss—Dora's interested stare be damned.

"I did, thank you. How about you? Is restaurant work all it's cracked up to be?"

"I was nervous at first, but Dora's been helping me and I'm getting the hang of it. Plus, I enjoy waiting on the customers. They're friendly and smile and thank me for bringing them their food. Finn and the others would throw it at me half time if it wasn't exactly how the liked it."

Vic grunted. "Yeah, well, most of our customers treat the staff well, but we have a few cranky ones here and there. Food-throwing is off-limits, though, so you should be safe from that."

Kellan pressed his cheek to Vic's chest. "I know you wouldn't let anyone do that to me."

Vid tried not to be too blatant as he scented the air. With each day that passed, Kellan's aroma became more pungent, more irresistible. He'd never been aware of the scent of birds before—except when they were cooked—but with Kellan, everything had changed. He might want to eat Kellan up, but not in the way he'd eaten birds before.

Vic snort-laughed at his errant thought then pulled back to look into Kellan's eyes. "Hey, as soon as the night shift guy gets here, I'll sit down and have dinner with you. Have you had a break at all yet?"

"No, I've been waiting for you."

"Kellan, you need to be careful while your ankle's still healing." Vic sighed. "I don't want you overdoing it."

"I won't, I promise. It hasn't been busy at all and anyway, I'm used to working very hard. This is a cinch." Kellan peered around Vic. "I'll be right back. Those guys at the counter might need more coffee."

Good idea. Might need some myself. "Okay, sweetheart. I'll be up front checking in with Dora."

Kellan froze, staring up at him with his lip trembling again.

Shit. What did I do now?

"Are you okay?"

Kellan sniffed. "You called me sweetheart."

Vic brushed back a strand of Kellan's hair that had come loose and was dangling across his forehead. "Well, that's what you are to me. Is that all right?"

He gave a shaky nod, pressing his lips together as if trying to keep control. "No one's ever said that about me before."

Vic stroked his cheek. "They do now." He pressed another quick kiss to Kellan's lips. "After you take care of those customers, you'll take a break with me, okay?"

"I will. Promise."

Vic wasn't sure how subtle he was being as he snuck an eyeful of Kellan's ass as he walked away, but it couldn't be helped. With an appreciative sigh, he turned his attention to Dora. She leaned against the register counter, her arms crossed and a smirk planted on her lips.

As her strolled toward her, he pretended not to notice. However, it appeared she wasn't about to let him off the hook that easy.

"Finally found the one, huh?"

Vic lifted his eyebrows. "It's *that* obvious?"

She chuckled. "Yup. On the rare occasion I've seen you with anyone, you would hustle them in and out of here so fast, I would barely catch a glimpse. Then, there's that one." She jerked her head in Kellan's direction. "All day long. 'Vic says this, Vic says that, Vic is so smart, Vic is so nice, blah blah blah'. I've known you for over five years and I don't think I've talked about you that much in *total*."

Heat filled Vic's cheeks. "He's just young and... he's been through a lot and... uh yeah, so anyway." He ran a hand across the top of his head. "You got a spool of thread and a couple needles up here?"

"*Excuse* me?"

"I thought it would be nice to string some cranberries with Kellan tonight, maybe put together some Thanksgiving center-pieces...what?"

She shook her head, chuckling. "Nothing, Vic. Just that love looks good on you."

CHAPTER SEVEN

Kellan finished filling the last set of shakers from his side work, more than ready to be done for the day. He didn't want to worry Vic, but his ankle had finally begun to twinge a bit. The pain would get better once he rested and used the heating pad, he was sure of it. *Better not worry Vic, though.* If he let his Alpha know he was hurting, that would be the end of him working at the restaurant. He'd be stuck in the hotel room for days and be bored out of his mind.

He held in a snicker. *Unless Vic spends it with me.* But he knew his responsible and practical mate wouldn't shirk his duties.

Which brought him to his next dilemma. As he carried the tray of completed shakers to the counter in order to place them at each setting, he wondered how he should broach the subject of his impending heat. Over the course of the evening as he'd struggled to keep his rock-hard dick from betraying his arousal and had resisted the urge to jump Vic in front of the dinner crowd, he'd realized what was going on.

When he'd met Vic in the beginning, the spark of attraction had been immediate. Then, he'd been charmed by how kind Vic was, by how much he enjoyed spending time with him. But he'd now reached the point where the only thing he cared about was Vic pounding into him over and over, so he could get rid of the unscratchable itch plaguing him.

Kellan bit his lip. *I'll worry about being an egg-layer later.* He doubted it would be an issue, however. He'd never heard of swans mating with wolves. *Or any other predator, for that matter.*

Vic emerged from the kitchen, talking over his shoulder as he pushed through the door. "I *am* serious about the you-know-whats, Skip. Can you make sure you take care of it first thing when you get in?"

Skip's booming voice carried through the now-closed door. "I still say you're gonna have them coming at you with pitchforks! I never heard of Christmas trout before!"

Vic rolled his eyes and let out a grunt.

Kellan hoped Skip was only yelling because of how he liked to be loud and that nothing was actually wrong. "Is he really mad at you?"

Vic tugged Kellan to his side. "Skip fears change, that's all. He'll get over it. Ready to call it a day?"

"Yeah." Kellan called forth all his nerve. "At least as far as the restaurant goes."

Vic's eyebrows shot up. "Did you have something else in mind?"

Kellan peered around the room. No customers remained, the closed sign was up, but the busser and Dora were still there. However, they seemed to be out of hearing range. *Looks safe.* "Can we go to your cabin and be alone together?"

"Oh." Vic furrowed his brow and for a horrifying moment, Kellan thought he might be rejected. Then Vic lowered his head and spoke in a low voice next to his ear. "Are you sure? I haven't been wanting to pressure you."

Kellan was aching for that kind of pressure. "I'm *so* sure that I think we should leave soon before I embarrass myself."

Vic's gaze traveled to the front where Dora stood counting down the register then adjusted himself. "Yeah, good plan. I might be in danger of similar embarrassment."

Kellan laughed, something he hadn't done much of in recent years. It felt damn good.

Vic smiled down at him. "That was a wonderful sound. I hope to give you reason to do it more often." He took Kellan's hand then brought it to his lips, kissing his knuckles. "We should go."

They said their goodnights to Dora and the busboy, then traveled hand in hand to Vic's cabin. They'd bundled up before leaving the restaurant, so they could take the outside entrance to the parking lot and go around the back to Vic's place. It would be Kellan's first time inside and the scheming, swan part of him wanted to finagle a way to never have to leave. However, the biggest part of him, the part that cared about and wanted to please his mate, would do no such thing. He'd let Vic take the lead.

Even if I was the teensiest bit pushy just now.

Right as they got to the long pathway that led up to Vic's cabin, Kellan lost his footing on a patch of ice. Vic scooped him up in his arms before he could land on the ground and it was almost the same as when Vic had rescued him.

Except that time, we were both naked.

Kellan rested his head against Vic's chest, allowing himself to be cradled by the strong man. Once Vic reached the entrance to his home, he shifted Kellan's weight to turn the door knob. He shouldered it open then carried Kellan to a long sofa placed in front of a river rock fireplace that bore a strong resemblance to the much larger one in the inn's lobby. After setting Kellan gently on the couch, Vic smiled down at him, brushing his hair back from his face before going back to shut the door.

"Rest your ankle while I fix us a fire."

Kellan knew he should be more nervous about what they were about to do, but instead, he craved it. His cock had been half-hard most of the day, threatening to betray him at every turn. But his longing was so much more than a passing lust.

At his core something had begun to build, something different than he'd ever experienced. He'd begun to change inside in a way he didn't understand. His heat wasn't a shock to him, he'd been expecting it to appear soon, considering his age. However, his body no longer seemed as if it belonged to him. It was as if he'd been taken over by a wanton creature who wanted nothing more than to present his ass for Vic to claim it. All he could think about was Vic fucking him, filling and stretching him wide open.

Kellan wiped away some beads of sweat that had formed on his upper lip. The room might be ice cold still, but he was bundled up in his coat and slowly being consumed by a desire he hadn't known could exist.

Vic replaced the fire poker on the stand then turned to face Kellan. He advanced toward him, predatory, but not in the way Kellan had feared in the beginning. Once he reached Kellan, Vic fell to his knees.

"I'll keep you warm, sweetheart. But let's get you out of these clothes." He met Kellan's gaze. "I'll be careful with you. We'll go slow."

Kellan shook his head. "No, not slow. I need you so much."

Vic rose on his knees, then wrapped his large hand around Kellan's nape, tugging him closer. "I need you, too. But I refuse to hurt you by being too eager."

Kellan tumbled onto Vic's lap. "You won't. I can... I can tell I'm getting slick, that I'm ready for you."

"That's not the only thing you'll need to make you ready for me." Vic offered him a soft smile. "No matter what, I'll make sure it's good."

As Vic pulled and tugged at his clothes, he placed soft kisses along Kellan's forehead, his jaw, his neck. Kellan moaned, rubbing his body against Vic's, the maddening urge to be mated clawing at him and reducing him to nothing but a wild thing demanding to be fucked raw.

Vic's caresses remained tender as he gentled him. Kellan fought his mate, tried to lure him into dispensing with the fore-play and driving into him instead.

"Shh, Kellan. We have all night."

They were both finally naked, so drawing things out any longer seemed ridiculous. Kellan straddled Vic's lap, grinding his heated length against Vic's. Kellan threw back his head, hissing at the glorious heat branding him where their hardened cocks met.

Ah, yes.

Time became nothing as he writhed on Vic's lap, every nerve in his body screaming and making him crazy. Vic ran his palms over Kellan's skin, touching and kneading him, driving his desire to a fevered pitch. Kellan let out a small whimper as Vic ghosted a finger over his twitching hole. He arched his back in a futile effort to force Vic to breach him.

"I know you're aching, sweetheart. But let me guide you so you don't get hurt."

Kellan collapsed against Vic's body, frustration threatening to tear him apart. He nuzzled Vic's face, his beard, then clamped his teeth onto Vic's earlobe and bit down hard. Vic let out a cry and swatted Kellan's ass.

"That's enough, love. Behave yourself. You won't goad me into penetrating you too soon."

Soon? Is he kidding?

"Vic, please. Inside me, *please.*"

This time when Vic touched his hole, he didn't pull away. He continued to tease Kellan's wrinkled opening, sparking sensations in him he'd never experienced. Vic captured his lips in a heated kiss, pushing his tongue into Kellan's mouth and exploring him thoroughly. Lost in their connection, of tasting his mate and sharing his breaths, he didn't realize until it had already happened that Vic had pushed one finger inside his ass.

He bore down, not caring that Vic wanted to control their exchange. Kellan no longer felt as if he were the same person. Nothing existed for him except the agonizing need threatening to consume him alive. As if sensing how lost Kellan had become, Vic introduced a second finger, the burn and stretch so satisfying.

More.

"My sweetheart..."

Vic pumped his fingers in and out of Kellan's passage while they traded kisses—their lips meeting then breaking free as they sought each other's skin, nibbling and tasting whatever flesh they could reach. As Kellan squirmed in Vic's lap, riding his fingers, he came, splashing his cum against Vic's belly.

Vic flipped Kellan around so his back was to him. Whatever mad lust that ruled over Kellan had now seemed to take hold of Vic as well. He lifted Kellan up by his hips then pressed the blunt head of his dick against Kellan's hole, pushing past his tight rim and spreading him impossibly wide. The initial resistance gave way as Kellan's slick helped ease Vic into his ass.

Because Vic had changed their position, Kellan was able to brace his forehead against the couch cushion. He grasped the edge and pushed back, taking more of Vic's thickness inside his body. They both let out a shared moan once he was fully seated. Vic held him still as if allowing him the chance to adjust to his girth.

Impaled on his mate's length and enveloped in a glorious burn, Kellan finally understood what the fuss was all about. His hunger wasn't completely sated, but he was closer than ever. Vic nipped at and licked his back, low growls rumbling from his chest as Vic began to thrust into his passage. Vic grasped Kellan's shoulder with one hand and gripped his waist with the other, holding him in place as he drove his cock into Kellan in an increasingly quicker pace.

Vic fucked him faster and harder, a fine sheen of sweat building where their flesh met, their skin slapping together with each plunge that shoved Kellan against the couch's edge. Vic froze, cocooning his frame around Kellan's back. He reached beneath them and grabbed Kellan's cock, stroking it with vigor as he shot his warm seed inside Kellan's passage. Kellan let out a strangled cry, coming at the same moment that Vic's cock seemed to swell at the base, spreading his rim more, then locking them in place.

"What's happening?"

Vic rubbed his nose along Kellan's shoulders and neck, scenting him as he continued to make low growling sounds.

"I'm knotting you. Filling you with my seed and keeping it there."

Kellan knew nothing of wolf mating rituals, but he'd never heard of swans doing such a thing. The pulsing in his ass from Vic's cock continued, the flutters pleasing. Being joined with his mate as if they were one was as wonderful as he'd imagined it would be. And while the edge had been taken off, he hoped Vic had been serious about them having the whole night ahead of them still.

Kellan had the feeling his heat was far from over.

CHAPTER EIGHT

*K*ellan groaned as he plopped down on the big arm chair in Vic's living room. A small smile formed on his lips. *My living room now too.* At the reminder of how amazing his life had become, his mood lifted. Kellan tugged off his boot, flakes of snow shaking off and landing on the rug. He'd worry about it later. Thanksgiving Day at the restaurant had been exhausting and all he wanted to do was spend the evening cuddling with Vic.

They did that a lot.

He slumped back in the chair and rubbed his belly. He felt so bloated from all the food he'd eaten. While he didn't think he'd had all that much, he must have. His tummy was even the slightest bit rounded.

A rush of cold air blew in as Vic entered. He'd ushered Kellan inside before him, telling him he'd grab another bundle of wood to add to the one they already had on the hearth. They both had the next day off and planned on locking themselves in the cabin and not leaving it for anything. Kellan had already set the box of leftovers on the kitchen table, and as soon as he get some circulation going again in his poor, sad toes, he'd take care of that as well as soaking up the now-melted snow water on the rug.

Kellan hissed as he wiggled his sore toes. *I should get the other boot off and take care of all this.* The firewood clattered as Vic added it to the rest of the logs. He straightened, rubbing his lower back and groaning. Vic turned around and chuckled, his gaze traveling to Kellan massaging his own feet.

"We're a mess." His features lit up. "Hey, I have an idea. Remember that bath bomb I got you at Grayson's shop? Did you ever use it?"

Kellan smiled. If things were moving in the direction he thought they were, then he highly approved. "No. I was saving it for something special."

"Would us soaking in a nice hot bath together be considered special?" Vic grinned, his sexy smile and smoldering gaze making Kellan all gooey inside.

"Absolutely. I forgot to take my boots off at the door again, but I'll clean it up and put the food away if you want to start the bath."

Vic glanced down at his own boots that still held the remnants of fresh powder on them, the rest having already melted away. "Don't worry about it. I tromp through here with them on all the time." He shrugged. "I think you've figured out by now that I'm not that stuck on everything being just so. A little mess here and there is no big deal to me."

Kellan lowered his head and chewed on his thumbnail. Things had been so busy at the restaurant and Skip had startled him while barking out some orders right next to his ear.

"Hey." Vic petted Kellan's hair. "Come on, I know what you're thinking. We've all dropped things at the restaurant, it's inevitable."

Kellan's shoulders slumped and he sighed. "Yeah, but I dropped a tray of plates piled with food. It went everywhere."

Vic kept caressing him as he chuckled. "It's okay, sweetheart. Skip needs to learn to dial it back on his thunderous bellowing."

Kellan peered up at the man who had changed his world into one filled with acceptance and love. "I'm glad you're my fated mate and not a swan. Every swan I've ever known, except for my mother, has been mean and selfish. I always thought there was something wrong with me because I wasn't that way. That's why Finn hated me so much. He equated caring with weakness."

Vic kneeled down on the floor in front of him and held him close. Kellan melted against Vic's frame, the wolf wrapping him in a comforting embrace. Even though his swan had feared the rugged man—had been certain Vic would tear him to pieces—Kellan had at last found the home in Vic's arms that had forever eluded him in his herd.

"You're everything I've ever dreamed of and more, sweetheart. Don't ever doubt that." Vic nuzzled his hair. "Does it bother you that I can't fertilize your eggs? I don't want you to regret staying with me when you could be with another swan and hatch young with them."

Kellan pulled back, drawing his eyebrows together. "But, you don't know that for sure. Why would we be fated mates if you can't fertilize my eggs? I think there's still a chance."

Vic's forehead wrinkled as he brushed Kellan's hair away from his face. "I want you no matter what else happens." He worried his lip. "Maybe I can ask Rosemary if she knows anyone who can help us."

Kellan tilted his head. "How could anyone help us?"

"She's been around a long time, has a lot of high-powered connections. Plus, Vale Valley has the top hospital in the country that specializes in male pregnancy. Surely, someone *has* to be knowledgeable in avian fertility issues."

A rush of hope surged through Kellan. The idea of laying egg after egg, only to discover they weren't fertile, would be agonizing to go through. And as an egg-layer who had just completed his first heat, there would be many years of eggs to come. Fortunately, as a shifter, his egg laying heat would only occur once a year, but he was young. The potential to have many children was there. *Or to have many crushing disappointments.* It would be awful for Vic to go through as well.

"Do you really think she might be able to help?"

Vic offered him a smile. "It can't hurt to ask, right?"

Kellan smiled back, the worry that had threatened to derail their romantic evening together becoming diffused by Vic's reassurances. "No, it sure can't. I bet she'd want to help us, too."

"I know she would. She's the heart of this town." Vic rose and offered Kellan his hand. "What do you say we enjoy that bath?"

Kellan allowed himself to be tugged to his feet. "I say yes. I'll go put the food away."

Vic wrapped his large hand around Kellan's nape then took a slow, thorough kiss. "Mmm. Be quick." As Kellan turned to make his way to the kitchen, Vic swatted his butt. "Don't make me wait."

With a much lighter heart, Kellan took care of the leftovers, ignoring how full he still felt. He and his mate would spend the night and the next day wrapped up in each other and that was all that mattered.

When he made his way into the bathroom with the big jacuzzi tub set in a waterproofed wood base, he spotted Vic sniffing the large, round bath bomb. He regarded Kellan as he entered the room.

"Two questions. Why are you still dressed and what the hell is ylang-ylang?"

Kellan snorted. "You asked me that before."

Vic drew his eyebrows together. "Which one?"

Kellan laughed. "Both, I think. But when we were at the aromatherapy shop, you wondered about the bomb. It's a type of flower. Do you like it? I know how sensitive you are to smell. We don't have to use it if you don't want to."

Vic took another sniff. "No, I actually like it quite a bit." He tossed it in the tub then jumped back as the bomb came to life in a noisy and colorful bout of fizzing. "Oh damn! It's not really gonna explode, is it?"

Streaks of purple, blue and fuschia bubbled and swirled together as Kellan grabbed his middle, laughing at how terrified his big bad wolf appeared over the bath accessory. "Oh my gods, you should see your face."

Vic looked at him then back at the now mellower bomb that had begun to peter out. The colors had mixed together into a reddish purple. He took a tentative step closer then peered over the edge. He turned to Kellan.

"Do you think it's safe to get in?"

Kellan had to wipe a tear from under his eye, Vic's reaction cracking him the hell up. "I promise, it's safe. I've never used a bomb before, but always wanted one. I love soaking in the water, obviously. But bath bombs and lakes don't go well together."

Vic approached him and started tugging at his clothes. "Then you can have as many as you want. We'll go back to Grayson's shop the next time I work out and you can choose a bunch of different ones to try."

"It will help with our aches too, because of the salts in it."

Vic slid Kellan's shirt off his shoulders as he glanced behind him. "Is that what all that sizzling was about?"

Kellan ran his fingers beneath Vic's flannel and tank, finding the six-pack of muscles covered in a swath of soft, dark hair. He quested higher up until he reached Vic's taut nipples, flicking them with his thumbs and loving the moan of pleasure it encouraged from Vic.

A low rumble built in Vic's chest. "Rest of the clothes off, now. Naked. Water."

Kellan grinned as he hurried to remove his pants and underwear. He'd noticed that the more aroused Vic was the less coherent he became.

That works for me.

Vic let out a long groan as he lowered himself slowly into the steaming bath. "Oh, fuck. Yeah, that's the stuff right there." He settled then raised his arms toward Kellan. "Come on, sweetheart. This feels so damn good."

Kellan accepted Vic's help and he let out his own groan of pleasure. The heat was like a comforting embrace and it immediately soothed his sore feet. He wiggled his toes again as he settled between Vic's legs, resting with his back to Vic's chest. Vic wrapped his arms around Kellan, his hands never still as they roamed his body, touching him everywhere he could reach.

Vic encircled Kellan's slender cock with his fist, lazily pumping his stiff length, neither of them in a hurry to get to their mutual destination. When he'd been under the spell of his heat, the frantic desperation had been intense and overwhelming. He'd loved every second of it. But taking his time with Vic, learning and exploring every inch of his mate—that was to be treasured.

Kellan let out a happy sigh. "I love you, Vic.

Vic hummed next to his ear. "I love you too, sweetheart."

∾

*V*ic squeezed the handle of the staple gun and with a *thwack*, the tail end of the red tinsel garland was attached to the ceiling. He set the gun down on the ledge of the stepladder then swiped the back of his hand across his forehead, careful not to topple over onto the lunch counter as he did. The decorations were finally completed in the restaurant and they'd done the lobby the day before, so that meant it was time to treat Kellan to some fun.

Me too.

It felt as though they'd been going almost non-stop since the week before Thanksgiving when the lead-up to the big day had begun. Kellan had begun to help with the baking in-between shifts and had taken to the decorating with glee. The tips of Kellan's fingers had their own unique decorations—tiny red dots from where they'd been poked with the needle. Sometimes, Vic would watch Kellan in amusement, sitting in a back booth peeling Super Glue off those same fingers at the end of the night. His creative and glittery Christmas wreaths were showcased in both the lobby and restaurant. Vic had needed to rein him in when he'd also wanted to do one for each room at the inn.

Vic climbed down from the ladder then folded it back up, returning both that and the gun to the storage closet. He washed his hands in the large utility sink next to the closet with what he was sure was a ridiculous smile plastered on his face. For the first time ever, he had a childlike excitement over going to the town's annual Christmas Market. Kellan had brought him alive.

As he made his way to what had become Kellan's personal work area in his favorite booth, he noted how Kellan was scrambling to clean up his craft supplies. Vic's smile grew wider.

He's as excited as I am.

"Hey, sweetheart. Are you about ready?"

Kellan grinned up at him as he shoved a plastic container of tiny ornaments into his craft tote. He'd been using them to decorate the mini trees he'd placed on the ledges connecting the backs of the booths. The dining room had never been so festive.

Or sparkly.

"Yeah. Two minutes, tops."

Vic helped gather up the rest of Kellan's things and soon they were off. They snuck through the hallway connecting the restaurant to the lobby and approached the front desk. Mark glanced up from the computer screen.

"Are you guys headed to the market?"

"We sure are." Vic rubbed his hands together. "I can't wait to get my hands on some of that peppermint fudge I've heard everyone talking about."

Mark smiled. "Oh yeah. That's from Sweet Bites' booth, isn't it? I haven't been there since they opened, have you?"

Vic wrapped an arm around Kellan's shoulders. "I took Kellan there the day they opened. You should give them a try. They have sweet and savory crepes. But the fudge is a special deal for the market only."

"Cool. Then I'd better get a night off, so I can go there and get some before it's all gone."

Vic smirked. "Funny. Next week, you have the whole weekend off. Then you can indulge all you want."

Kellan cleared his throat and moved out of Vic's embrace. "Um, Mark, is it okay if I put my bag behind the desk for now?"

"Sure, Kel. You don't have to ask."

"Thank you." Kellan ducked his head then gingerly moved behind the counter, placing his bag next to the cabinet that held all the lobby brochures and office supplies.

Vic exchanged a glance with Mark, jerking his chin one time. Kellan had come a long way when it came to being less nervous around Mark, but they weren't best buddies quite yet, either.

"Okay, let's go. I need a sugar fix."

Kellan's bright smile returned, and Vic extended his hand. After saying goodnight to Mark, they headed to the truck, the excitement over their holiday outing palpable. They were fortunate the night was clear and that it hadn't snowed in almost a week. The roads were plowed, the town square where the market was held would be bustling, and nothing would prevent the live musicians from playing Christmas Carols as a backdrop to the evening.

As they drove toward the center of town, the multitude of

Christmas lights made Kellan 'ooh' and 'ah' the same as it had the night of the tree lighting ceremony. Vic tried not to let his thoughts drift to the possibility of them being childless, but all he could think of in the moment was what a wonderful parent Kellan would make, that he'd be the type of dad who would share in all sorts of fun activities with their kids.

Vic forced his thoughts back to the present. The night was about him and Kellan, about them being together and enjoying the fun and excitement of the season.

"Oh look, we're in luck."

Vic steered the truck into a parking spot right as another vehicle pulled out. The passenger side would be next to the snow berm, but if the door didn't clear it, Kellan could climb out the driver's side. Vic shut off the engine and angled his body toward him.

"Can you get the door open?"

Kellan tugged on the handle and the door made it halfway before meeting the resistance of the solid, packed snow. "I can squeeze out."

"Hold on. Let me help you."

After Vic dropped out of the truck, he came around to lift Kellan over the berm before placing him on the cleared street. He gave him a kiss then gathered up his gloved hand into his as they strolled toward the market. Vic had managed to get a spot only about a block away, so already they could hear the music floating on the air.

Once they set foot on the square lined with booths on all sides, Kellan stopped, causing Vic to come to a halt as well. Kellan gazed around the opulent displays while Vic enjoyed watching the excitement in his eyes. Every booth was lit up and decorated with their own theme—some with boughs of pine that sported red and gold bows, others with wreaths of holly accented with miniature white twinkling lights and one booth was even encased entirely in red and white striped ribbon as if it were a giant candy cane. The festive stalls offered up a myriad of items. Handcrafted wooden toys in one, silver and gold jewelry in another, one with quilts and handmade baby clothes along with a booth of outfits for pets—something for everyone

Kellan pointed. "Oh look! Creatures of Comfort is here, there's Flora. It looks like they have some candles too." He peered up at him. "I bet they're scented." Kellan tugged on Vic's hand. "We should also check to see if they have any special bath bombs for the holidays."

Vic laughed as Kellan eagerly pulled his hand and dragged him toward Grayson's booth. While Kellan perused the offerings, Vic glanced around the bustling and happy crowd. Then someone caught his eye. He furrowed his brow, stretching his neck as he tried to peek through the clusters of shoppers to get a better look at the familiar face.

Wait. Is that Mateo? He squinted his eyes then widened them again in surprise. *With Father Lance? No way.* Not that a priest couldn't enjoy the Christmas market along with everyone else, but they seemed *awfully* cozy together. *I need to drop by the tattoo shop this week.* He planned on hunting for some details.

Kellan grabbing his sleeve knocked him out of his reverie. "Which one do you think we should get? There's mocha latte fusion and strawberry crème surprise."

Kellan held up two large bath bombs—one a light brown with cream-colored swirls and a pale pink one with similar swirls. Vic took a tentative sniff of them both, his mouth watering at how delicious they smelled.

"What's the surprise?"

Flora giggled. "If I told you, it wouldn't be one. But I can give you a hint. We put coupons for things like free massages inside a capsule that's revealed once the bomb dissolves. You never know what you might get."

Vic arched his eyebrows. "Dude. That's cool." He regarded Kellan. "Do you like both of them?"

Kellan nodded with a big smile. Vic turned to Flora.

"Sold."

Kellan went up on his toes, placing a hand on Vic's shoulder to support himself as he whispered in Vic's ear. "They have the same scents for the candles too."

Vic chuckled. "Pick out the ones you want, and we'll get those too."

Kellan turned his face up for a kiss and Vic happily obliged.

As Flora wrapped their purchases in shiny gold paper, Grayson showed up with a box full of more merchandise. He set the overloaded container on the back table then turned to face them with a wide smile.

"Merry Christmas, guys." He regarded Kellan. "Enjoying our town market?"

"It's amazing. We just got here, but I can already tell I'm going to love it."

"Good, I'm glad." Grayson turned to Vic. "Things picking up at the inn yet?"

"Oh yeah, it's been going great. We even have some psychic investigator staying with us who's doing a show." Vic rolled his eyes. "One of my front desk guys got involved with the proceedings somehow, but I'm staying out of that whole thing."

Grayson chuckled. "Yeah, my grandmother was telling me about it." He winked. "As long as none of the town's *true* secrets are revealed."

"I bet Rosemary is on it."

Grayson raised one eyebrow. "Trust me. She is."

Once he'd paid for their goodies and Flora had finished bagging them up, they asked Grayson to give their regards to his grandmother. They continued down the aisle to the next booth. Vic wrapped an arm around Kellan's shoulders. He loved his town and the shifters, witches and humans were great, but dammit, Kellan was *his*. Despite how irrational the idea that everyone intended to steal his beautiful mate out from under him truly was, he couldn't help it.

Every once in a while, Kellan would stop to tell one of the vendors how incredible one of their items was or point out something he thought Vic would like. They reached the end of the first row and Vic spotted Sweet Bite's booth. The line to get the already notorious fudge was at least ten people deep.

"Uh oh." Vic nudged Kellan's shoulder. "We'd better get over there before it's all gone."

Kellan gasped. "You're right!"

Vic grabbed Kellan's arm before he could take off. "Why don't you wait in line and I'll go buy us some hot cocoa."

Vic laughed as Kellan jetted over to the booth the instant he'd released his hold. Since the hot cocoa stand was one of the most popular stops every year at the market, there was plenty of extra help on hand. Spiced eggnog, hot apple cider and plain ol' coffee was also available for those who preferred something other than the decadent chocolate drink topped with whipped cream.

After he'd purchased their cocoa—complete with a mini candy cane as a stirrer—he made his way back to Kellan. Only two more customers to go and it would be their turn, so he'd returned just in time.

"Here you go, sweetheart."

Kellan set his Creatures of Comfort bag down and accepted the steaming drink from him. "Oh, it's so pretty."

"Be careful." Vic chuckled. "I've burned my tongue more than once on this stuff."

"Okay, I'll eat the cream first."

Kellan proceeded to scoop up the white fluff with the candy stick, sucking the cream off then licking his lips. He made small noises of pleasure then went in for round two.

Vic clenched his jaw to hold in a groan. *He's trying to kill me.*

At last, Kellan had finished fellating the candy cane and it was their turn at the booth. Vic purchased a half pound for them then picked up three more for the staff Christmas party that was coming up that week.

They wandered to the next aisle, sipping their cooling cocoa and enjoying the lights and decorations as much as the wares. Kellan gasped then shoved his almost empty cup at Vic before rushing to a stall a few booths away.

What the hell?

He caught up to Kellan right as he picked up a stuffed wolf, holding the toy in front of him and staring at it with an expression of adoration. Vic froze, glued to the spot, unable to tear his eyes from the scene before him. He swallowed past a lump in his throat, his eyes burning as he committed the moment to memory where he could add it to the many other wonderful ones he'd been building with Kellan.

Kellan turned to him, his jaw slack. "Oh Vic, can we please get it? The markings and the color of the coat is almost exactly like yours!"

Vic coughed into his fist in an effort to regain control of himself. "Of course, you can have it." He stooped down to press a kiss to Kellan's temple. "And you've got the real thing too, forever and ever."

Kellan hugged the wolf to his chest. "You're much better than any stuffed toy, but I was thinking that if any of my eggs should ever be fertile and we have a baby, they'd love it too."

Vic sniffed and swiped a finger under his eye, unable to respond other than to nod. He waved his hand toward the woman manning the booth, hoping that Kellan would get the message that he should give it to her so they could pay. He pushed a couple bills into Kellan's palm then dipped his head back in a bid to keep the tears from spilling.

Kellan tugged on his hand and Vic noted that the toy had been wrapped in red and green tissue inside a gift bag, the very end of its snout peeking out from beneath the folds of paper. He beamed a smile up at Vic.

"Thank you, Vic. We can put it under the tree and save it for Christmas morning."

Oh gods. He's gonna get me all wound up again.

Since he didn't want to be caught openly weeping in the middle of the town square, he decided to take a moment and haul all their purchases to the truck so he could pull himself together. Vic left Kellan with Flora for a bit, since he loved to quiz her about the different oils and what they were used for.

When he returned, Flora was helping a customer and Kellan was standing off to the side, holding his palm against his belly with an odd expression. Vic hurried over to him.

"Hey, what's wrong?"

He gave a slight shake of his head. "I'm not sure. You know how I keep getting full really fast all the time when I eat?"

"Yeah."

"Well, that came on all of a sudden as well as a kind of gurgling in my gut. But all I had was the cocoa."

Vic frowned. "Maybe it was the whipped cream. You did eat that kind of fast." *Boy, did you ever.* "If you're feeling bad, we can leave. We can pick up some ginger ale on the way home."

"No, I don't want to go." Kellan regarded him with imploring eyes. "It's better now. I was just surprised, that's all."

"Are you sure? There's still another weekend left before Christmas, we could come back again."

Kellan clutched his hand. "But what if there's another storm? It's so pretty tonight, we can see the stars. And we haven't even watched the ice skaters yet."

Vic pulled Kellan into his arms. "All right, let's stay. But if your stomach starts bothering you again, then let me know." Vic framed Kellan's face between his gloved hands. "I love you and you're very precious to me."

Kellan offered him a wide smile. "I love you too, lots and lots. Can we go to the rink now?"

Vic rubbed their cold noses together. "Anything you want, sweetheart."

CHAPTER NINE

*V*ic trudged across the parking lot, exhausted from a load of craziness at both the inn and restaurant. One of his staff members from housekeeping, Lila, had fallen into some bizarre coma with zero explanation. Then, one half of the burners on the grill had died. With Christmas and the other year-end holidays upon them, he couldn't afford to have his kitchen compromised in any way.

When he reached the porch of his cabin, he banged the toes of his boots against the wood to shake off as much moisture and detritus as he could. He swung the door open and was in the middle of pulling off his gloves when Kellan burst from the bedroom at the back of the house, screeching and flapping his arms. Whoever thought mute swans were unable to make noise had never been around Kellan when he was either having sex or excited about something and speaking at the top of his lungs. This display, however, was something new altogether.

Kellan had made it halfway across the length of the cabin at full speed, when he seemed to come to his senses, grabbing hold of the couch arm to halt his progress. He let out a few puffs of air as his frantic breathing gradually slowed.

"Vic!" He placed a hand to his forehead. "Oh no, I'm so sorry. I don't know what came over me."

Vic was about to respond when he noticed that every cabinet and closet door within his visual range was wide open. He frowned as he finished removing his gloves, stuffing them in his coat pocket before shrugging it off. Once he'd tossed it on the coat hook, he took a few tentative steps toward Kellan. When he reached what he thought was a safe distance in case Kellan went berserk again, he opened his arms.

Kellan's lower lip trembled for a moment then he launched himself into Vic's embrace. He broke into fits of sobs.

"I-I'm sorry, p-please don't be m-mad. I l-love you so much, but it keeps going flat and I-I-I..." He hiccupped and tipped his head back and locked eyes with Vic, tears streaming down his face. "I don't know what's *wrong* with me. I thought you were dangerous and I like blacked out or something. All I could think of was beating someone's face in and pecking their eyes out."

Damn. His sweet swan had a quite a streak in him. Then, a wild image of Finn and the herd of gangster swans showing up in town flashed through his mind. "Do you think someone's coming to get you?"

"Not me. The *egg*. But I'm not worried about anyone in particular."

Vic tensed, his stomach tightening in anticipation. "You laid an egg!"

Kellan's lip trembled again, and he shook his head. "That's just it. There's no egg. Nothing. My belly still feels hard the way it's been for a while, so no big change there. But I have to get the blankets right and there's not enough of them. And the towels are too scratchy. I need extra thick, plushy ones that are nice and soft. Oh, and snails. I need lots and lots of snails."

"*S*nails?" Vic pulled his lips back in a grimace. "What do you need those for?"

Kellan inclined his head as he drew his eyebrows together. "To eat. I'm *starving*."

Gross.

"Uh, okay." Vic laced his fingers with Kellan and gently led him to the sofa. "Come on, sweetheart. Why don't you sit here on my lap and we'll figure all this out together."

"Thanks, Vic." He climbed onto Vic's thighs then wrapped his arms around Vic's shoulders. "I need you most of all. No one ever helped me, explained what an egg-layer is supposed to do. I was so young when my mom died that she never had a chance to prepare me." He regarded Vic. "What if there's something else I should be doing for the egg? What if I'm at the restaurant and the egg suddenly comes then?"

"Uh..." Vic had the sudden urge to visit Rosemary. *I wonder if she could use an apple pie right about now?* "Let's take this one step at a time." He cleared his throat. "Can you show me what you mean about the blankets going flat?"

"Sure."

Kellan hopped off Vic's lap then gestured for him to follow. As soon as Vic stepped through the threshold of the bedroom, he could see what Kellan meant. In the middle of their king-sized bed was a jumble of blankets all bunched together. They'd been shaped into a vague representation of a bowl, the middle of the pile showing a slight depression. But he could see what Kellan meant. A couple sides had sagged, and it appeared to Vic that every time Kellan had tried to smoosh the stiff, wool coverings into a circle, one of the other areas would flop over then fall flat. He rubbed his chin through his beard.

"Well, I'm certainly no expert at nest building, but maybe if we got some long pillows, you know, like those back-support kinds, we could make a frame. Then, we could get a bunch of softer blankets, maybe a puffy comforter as a base, and fill the middle section. All you'd have to do then was make a depression in the middle to…" He scratched his head. "To do whatever it is you need to do."

Kellan wiped his face with the back of his hand and let out another hiccup. He glanced up at Vic. "That would be perfect! I'm sure I could make that work." His shoulders drooped. "I'm sorry I'm causing so much trouble."

Vic scooped up a surprised Kellan in his arms and gave him a big kiss. He set him back on his feet but couldn't stop touching him, couldn't still his hands as he stroked his back and ran his fingers through Kellan's hair.

"How could you call getting ready for your egg trouble? This is incredible."

Kellan pressed his cheek to Vic's chest, clutching at his shirt. "Our egg. This is *our* egg." He sniffed. "At least, I hope there's an egg." He peered up at Vic. "Otherwise, why am I so compelled to build a nest?"

"Maybe that's your answer, then. Your instincts are leading you and even though another swan isn't here to guide you, you'll know what to do when the time comes."

Kellan seemed to ponder Vic's words, but the doubt clouding his features hadn't faded. Vic squeezed his shoulders, offering him what he hoped was an encouraging smile. Never had he been so out of his element on anything.

Rosemary. Pie.

"Hey, I have an idea. Why don't I run out and buy a bunch of blankets and pillows, then when I get back, I'll help you." He frowned. "Or is that something I'm not supposed to interfere with?"

"You can help. The egg-layer does most of the actual building, but the mate usually gets materials for the nest, so this is perfect." He sighed. "I feel a little better. Thank you, Vic." Kellan glanced at the pile on the bed again. "Oh, the towels. I want to line the inside with cushy, soft towels."

"You've got it. Plenty of towels, too."

Kellan followed Vic as he made his way back to the front of the cabin to put on his outerwear again.

"And don't forget the snails. I can't stop thinking about them."

Vic tried not to make a gagging noise. "I'll do the best I can. I'm not sure where to get anything like that, especially this time of year."

"You don't have any frozen ones in the restaurant?"

"Not last time I checked."

Skip's gonna love this. His cook still wouldn't shut up about the damn ducks.

Kellan furrowed his brow and rubbed a finger across his lower lip. "I'm *dying* for some good pond snails, but if I had to, I could make do with a couple juicy bullfrogs."

That's it. I'm never eating again.

"I might have better luck with the frogs. There's a specialty market in town that I've sometimes seen them in."

"You're the best mate ever, Vic. I don't know what I'd do without you."

More sobbing seemed imminent, so Vic gathered Kellan in his arms, whispering soothing words and gentling him before he dared leave his emotional mate alone, so he could embark on his mission.

"Okay, sweetheart. I'd better get going before it gets too late. Do you think you can rest a bit while I'm gone? Make sure you have lots of strength for the nest-building later?"

Kellan swiped a finger under his nose. "I can try. I sort of feel weird again like I did that night at the market."

Vic struggled between staying with Kellan if he wasn't feeling well or getting the blankets—*and snails*—for his agitated mate.

But Vic sensed that Kellan needed to focus on assembling his nest and, if he was having a craving, Vic could at least try to get him what he wanted.

"I'll be back as quick as I can."

After another kiss and hug, Vic took off. He jumped in his truck and headed to the restaurant to get an apple pie. While he hated to barge in on Rosemary, this was an emergency as far as he was concerned. He hoped the pie would soften the blow of his intrusion.

Once he reached her white, stately mansion that boasted three stories, he grabbed the pie offering and strode to her door with purpose. He attempted to maintain focus instead of obsessing over whether Kellan was at the cabin laying an egg with no one there to hold his hand.

Or whatever it is that swans do.

He smoothed a hand down his shirt them knocked on the door. Rosemary's maid, Philomena, answered almost immediately.

"Good evening, Vic. How are you?"

"Hi, Philomena. I'm okay. Listen, I hate to bother Rosemary at home, but do you think you could see if she'll speak with me? I promise I won't take up too much of her time."

"Well... she did just finish dinner."

Vic held up the pie triumphantly. "Perfect! I have her favorite apple pie."

Philomena let out a light laugh. "I'm sure that'll buy you an audience. Hold on a moment, Vic. I'll see if she's available."

To his extreme relief, Philomena returned not even a few minutes later and ushered him inside. He was led to what he remembered from a previous visit as being the drawing room. Rosemary breezed in right after.

"Ah Vic, I presume you've stopped by with some questions about that dear mate of yours?"

Vic twisted his hands, surprisingly nervous. If she didn't give him some info about their situation, he wasn't sure what he could do next. "Yeah, thanks so much for seeing me. I'm at my wit's end."

Rosemary gestured to the antique carved wood sofa with embroidered upholstery. "Have a seat, Vic. You're putting me on edge. When a fellow werewolf begins to come unhinged, it's rather disconcerting. The scent of fear is pouring off you."

Vic winced. "Oh. My bad." He perched on the edge of the couch.

She sighed then took the wing chair opposite him. "Now, what can I help you with?"

"His heat's over, I'm sure of that."

Rosemary snorted. "By 'his', I take it you mean Kellan?"

Vic rubbed his forehead. "Yeah, sorry, I'm so worried about him."

"Now, now, dear. Take a deep breath. Swans have been laying eggs for centuries and wolves have been whelping just as long." She shrugged. "Or thereabouts. Point being, the birth parent knows what to do—it's a built-in mechanism."

"Yeah, but most shifters here use the hospital these days and..." He clasped his hands together to keep from fidgeting. "Well, this is a swan and wolf all mixed up together." He frowned. "Maybe. We're afraid that if he does lay an egg, it won't be fertile because of me."

"Ah, I see. Well, we've had plenty of inter-specie shifter children before."

Vic sighed. "I'm not trying to argue with you, but, those have always been mammals and mammals, or..." He tried to remember if there were any avian and avian shifter pairs he knew of.

Rosemary crossed her arms and pursed her lips. "You seem to have forgotten about my grandchildren. Which is puzzling, since you're good friends with one of them."

Vic blinked a few times. *Oh shit. Right.* "I guess I was somehow equating merpeople with being more mammalian than anything else?" He offered her a smile, hoping it appeared as innocent as he was attempting to make it.

She rolled her eyes. "Good try. Let's get back to Kellan. You say he's done with his heat?"

"Yeah, a while ago. We assumed nothing would happen at all, you know, wolf and swan. But he's been feeling full a lot even when he barely eats, his belly is slightly rounded and a couple times, tonight included, he said his gut was gurgling and he felt funny. However, this whole time, he still hasn't been able to shift. I'm worried he might be sick or that something is really wrong."

Rosemary drew her eyebrows together. "Hmm. I only personally knew one pair of swan shifters and this was, oh my, over twenty years ago before they moved to Canada. They had three of the most adorable cygnets, such little darlings. But other than knowing through them that they couldn't shift when they were in heat, I don't know much else. I couldn't tell you whether Kellan still being unable to shift after so long is normal or not."

Vic dropped his head in his hands, a shroud of hopelessness enveloping him. He was failing Kellan, but not finding the answers that would give him reassurance that everything would be okay.

"Vic, don't despair."

Vic lifted his head and gaped at her. "How can you say that? You should've seen him tonight. He'd been tearing through the house before I got there, dragging every blanket and towel he could find out of the closets and trying to arrange a nest on the bed. He almost attacked me when I walked in the front door. I've never witnessed anything like it."

Rosemary had the nerve to chuckle. "It certainly sounds as if he's ready to lay an egg."

"But..." He didn't know what else to say to make her understand. Kellan might be able to lay an egg, but it might never hatch. And if Kellan never shifted again, he would likely die. No shifter could survive solely in human form forever.

He started at the touch of Rosemary's hand on his knee as she sat down next to him. "Listen, dear. I know of an avian fertility specialist only a few hours from here. What if I call him up, find out if he can come see Kellan, or if nothing else, give you a phone consultation?"

Vic grabbed Rosemary in a tight hug. "Oh gods, thank you, thank you *so* much." He released the visibly startled woman. "I'll never forget this. Free apple pie forever."

She laughed. "You're very welcome. Now, I have to take care of some business, so is that all I can help you with?"

"Actually," He gave her a lopsided grin. "I don't suppose you know where I can get lots and lots of pond snails?"

CHAPTER TEN

*K*ellan rubbed his hard abdomen, the sensation that he'd swallowed a bowling ball getting worse over the past twenty-four hours. It had been almost a week since Vic had sought out Rosemary's help. *Surely that bird guy should have come here by now?*

He considered the glass of beet and spinach juice he'd poured from the batch he'd pressed earlier and wrinkled his nose. Even though his stomach rumbled with hunger, he didn't think he had enough room in his tummy for even one drop. He set the glass in the refrigerator in case he wanted it later. If something didn't change soon, he'd faint from starvation.

Kellan pulled Vic's flannel robe more tightly around him. The scent of his mate was a comfort. Not being able to work by Vic's side everyday the way he'd been doing almost since he'd arrived in Vale Valley had left him so melancholy. But ever since that day when he'd become crazed with the need to build his nest, he hadn't wanted to be far from it and Vic had supported him in that decision. Vic had said it would ease his mind to know that Kellan was safe in the house and near his nest.

He smiled to himself as he made his way into the bedroom to curl up in the blankets and take a nap. Vic had been so right about the pillows and softer blankets. The nest had turned out perfect.

Right as Kellan was about to climb onto the bed, he froze, his senses on alert. His body tensed and white-hot anger surged through him. Someone was near.

Near my nest. Not my mate. Stranger!

Kellan hissed and snarled as he raced toward the front door, his only thoughts ones of murder. He'd claw and tear and bite at anyone who entered, anyone who *dared* to invade his home, to jeopardize his nest.

The door opened and he let out a high-pitched shriek, flapping his arms as he hopped from the couch to the chair to the coffee table then back to the couch. He screeched again, his throat raw from his howling as a strange man entered the room. Before he could register that Vic stood beside the stranger, he'd hurled himself at the unknown man and was snapping his teeth and clawing at his face.

He was yanked back by his waist, the man covering his face with his arms as Kellan hissed and struggled within the hold ofs whoever had pulled him away.

"Sweetheart, stop! It's me, calm down, everything's okay. No one's going to touch your nest, I promise."

Kellan gulped in huge mouthfuls of air, his heart thundering as he tried to make sense of what was happening.

Vic. Vic's here.

He blinked repeatedly as he gradually returned to awareness. His swan remained on high alert, ready to attack at the merest hint of a threat, but the adrenaline spike was already beginning to wear off.

"Vic? What's going on?"

Kellan turned in Vic's embrace, nuzzling his neck, breathing in his mate. Vic rubbed his back and after a few minutes, he relaxed in his hold. He peered over his shoulder, narrowing his eyes at the strange man who was dabbing at his cheek with a tissue. The man appeared to be in his fifties, with salt and pepper hair and a slash of red against his pale cheek where Kellan had gotten in a good strike. Kellan considered apologizing, but first, he'd wait and see who the man was and why he was invading his territory.

"Well," the man said with a final dab at his cheek. "I'd say he's ready to lay any time now."

Kellan turned back to Vic and frowned. "Who's he?"

"He's Dr. Arthur, the avian fertility specialist." Vic chuckled. "That was quite impressive."

Oh no. Kellan's cheeks filled with heat. Just the person he wanted to see, and he'd gone and attacked him. An apology was definitely needed. He turned back around and regarded Dr. Arthur.

"I'm so sorry, Dr. Arthur. When I think someone is going to hurt the nest, I lose control like that."

Dr. Arthur made a shooing gesture with his hand. "Think nothing of it. I was originally an ornithologist for years. Then I was turned by my mate, an eagle shifter. Trust me, I know *all* about nest protection behavior."

Kellan let out a relieved sigh. He was afraid he might have made Dr. Arthur so angry, he wouldn't agree to help them.

Vic cleared his throat. "Dr. Arthur? Won't you join us in the living room?"

Once they'd all gotten settled, with Kellan pressed to Vic's side on the couch and Dr. Arthur on the matching side chair perpendicular to them, he leaned forward with his hands clasped, offering Kellan a smile.

"Vic tells me you haven't shifted since early November and you had your first heat soon after, correct?"

He nodded. "That's right."

Dr. Arthur continued to verify different bits of information, including some embarrassing revelations regarding his and Vic's sexual activity. He jotted each revelation down in a tiny notebook he'd pulled from his jacket pocket.

"One last question, Kellan. Would it be all right with you if I felt your abdomen? I'd also like to listen to it with my stethoscope."

A rumbling growl came from deep within Vic's chest. Kellan glanced up at him in question. After all, it *was* Vic who had sought Dr. Arthur's help.

Vic squirmed on the couch. "Sorry. I'm a tad possessive. But if it's all right with Kellan, I think you should."

Kellan regarded Dr. Arthur. He didn't want a stranger touching him, but he wanted to know if his egg was okay even more. "Go ahead."

Kellan rested against the back of the couch and untied Vic's robe, letting it fall open. He mused how lucky he was that he hadn't fallen flat on his face with all the jumping around he'd done in the robe that was much too long for him. He lifted the hem of the dancing reindeer T-shirt he'd bought in the restaurant's gift shop and exposed his belly.

An undignified giggle-snort burst out of him at the first press of Dr. Arthur's cold fingers to his skin. He poked and prodded above and below Kellan's navel, finally hitting the most solid area at the pit of his abdomen, the pressure making Kellan uncomfortable to the point of wanting to vomit. He was about to ask Dr. Arthur to stop when the specialist pulled his hands away.

"That was fine, Kellan. Now I'll take a listen."

Kellan started at the first contact of the cold instrument to his belly and he clenched his fists. He hated waiting. That's all he'd been doing since he'd first realized he must be carrying an egg. Why couldn't Dr. Arthur hurry up?

Dr. Arthur scrunched his eyebrows together, nodding as he listened here, then there, then another spot entirely. "Hmm." He nodded some more then straightened. The smile he radiated back at them had Kellan's heart soaring even before he began to speak. "I can hear your baby's heartbeat. The egg is most definitely fertile."

Kellan squealed—a happy noise instead of a vicious one—and threw his arms around Vic's neck. Vic hugged him close, rocking him and whispering in Kellan's ear how happy he was, how he couldn't wait until their baby was hatched.

That's right.

Kellan twisted in Vic's embrace to face Dr. Arthur. "How far along am I, or however that gets worked out."

Dr. Arthur's eyebrows shot up. "Don't you know the basics of your egg-hatching cycle?"

Kellan shook his head. "No. I was the only egg-layer in my herd. An egg-layer was a liability for them once they'd decided to move around the country, making their way through life by robbing people. The only reason my brother put up with me at all was because we were related. At least I think that's why."

The blood seemed to drain from his body as a horrible realization came to him. Maybe Finn had planned on abandoning him all along. Perhaps Finn had known he was approaching his heat and didn't want him dragging down the herd. He hung his head.

"Sweetheart?" Vic encouraged him to look in his eyes. "Aren't you happy about the egg?"

What's wrong with me? Finn did me a favor. "The happiest I've *ever* been, Vic. I don't care about Finn or my herd or any of that anymore. They were never my true family, but you are. And Vale Valley is my genuine home. The beginning of the best day of my life was when Finn pushed me out of that truck. Now I have more joy than I'd ever dreamed possible."

Vic claimed his mouth in a deep kiss and it wasn't until Dr. Arthur loudly cleared his throat that they were pulled from their private world.

Kellan wiped the back of his hand across his lips. "Um, excuse us."

Vic chuckled. "I think he understands."

Dr. Arthur smiled, his eyes bright. "Oh, I do. But I believe you were wondering about timelines?"

"Oh!" Kellan straightened on the couch, tugging the robe back around him. "Yes. Since the egg is...is.." *Oh damn, here I go again. I refuse to cry.* If the egg was behind all the waterworks he'd been experiencing lately, then he hoped he'd be back to normal after the baby had hatched.

Baby...

Dr. Arthur leaned in, his eyebrows arched as he waited for Kellan to continue. Vic spoke up.

"I think what we're both wondering, is when will he lay the egg and how soon after that will it hatch?"

Dr. Arthur chuckled. "Excited parents, that's a wonderful thing. Since this is his first clutch, it could take longer. By all appearances, he should lay at any minute. The hatching should be approximately four to five weeks after."

Vic's arm tightened around him. "When you say 'clutch', will he lay more than one egg?"

"Sorry, I'm so accustomed to the terminology. I only detected one heartbeat and it's typical for a first clutch to either have one or two eggs or infertile ones. If you fertilize him again in the future, you could end up with a few viable eggs." He winked. "You might want to take that into consideration before you try for any more children."

Kellan tensed right along with Vic. "But...the egg is for sure fertile?" Vic absent-mindedly stroked Kellan's arm.

Dr. Arthur rose from the chair, his smile broad as he considered them both. "Yes, no worries there. However, I'm afraid I have to go. It's a bit of a drive back and I hear another storm is headed this way."

Vic stood and shook Dr. Arthur's hand. "Thank you so much, this has meant the world to both of us."

"You're welcome. I'm sure it comes as a relief." Dr. Arthur peered around Vic and gave Kellan a nod. "Congratulations. I know you're going to be a fantastic daddy."

Kellan grinned. The reality was finally sinking in. "Thanks." His gaze darted to the scratch he'd left on Dr. Arthur's skin. "And I didn't mean to hurt you, I'm sorry."

Dr. Arthur touched his fingers to his cheek. "Oh, that. I'd forgotten about it already." He made his way to the door then turned around as he was crossing the threshold. "Goodbye to you both. Call if you have any other questions, but I'm sure you'll do fine."

After he'd left, Vic returned to his side, but this time when he sat on the couch, he gathered Kellan onto his lap. "I'm not leaving this cabin again until you've laid your egg."

Kellan snuggled up to Vic. "*Our* egg, remember?"

"Mmm. Our baby." Vic buried his nose in Kellan's hair. "This is all so surreal, but I couldn't be more thrilled."

They held each other in silence, the only sound being the rustle of the branches in the light wind and the crackle of the well-seasoned wood in the fireplace. Part of what Vic had said sunk in.

"Hey, Vic?"

"Yeah?"

"You can't stay here round the clock with it being so busy at the inn and everything. It's Christmas week. I've heard you say plenty of times that it gets crazy between now and New Year's Day."

Vic tightened his hold. "I don't care."

Kellan rolled his eyes. "But it's not fair to everyone else. It's bad enough that I'm not there helping as it is." He glanced up at Vic. "And what about food?" They took most of their meals at the restaurant since it was so convenient.

Vic stuck out his lower lip. "I'll make Dora deliver them to the cabin."

Kellan sighed. "Vic, you're not being reasonable."

He huffed. "Reasonable? Who cares about *reasonable*? My mate is about to lay an egg at any minute!"

Kellan let out a laugh, then grabbed his abdomen. It didn't hurt, but it sure as hell felt weird. *Too much pressure.*

Vic gasped, grabbing Kellan's upper arms then holding him back, his gaze roaming Kellan's body. "Is it time? Should you go lie down in the nest?"

This is going to be fun.

"Vic, I'm fine, really. It's only that heavy feeling, the one I've had the past couple weeks. I mean, it's been getting gradually more intense, but other than that, everything else is the same."

Vic pressed his lips together. "That does it. I'm not leaving this cabin until that egg is laid."

Kellan flopped against his stubborn wolf. He stared into the fireplace, restless. He wanted Vic with him all the time, that wasn't the issue. But now it seemed as if all he'd be doing was watching and waiting for him to pop.

"Hey, I have an idea." Kellan angled his body to face Vic again. "What if you leave your cell phone with me? You're going to be *right there*, within walking distance. I'll call the front desk if anything happens."

Vic frowned. "*Walking* distance? You'd better not do any walking, that egg could fall right out of you!"

Kellan smacked his forehead. "First off, that's ridiculous. It doesn't work like that. But that wasn't what I meant. I was talking about it being walking distance for *you*." He stroked Vic's cheek, petting the soft beard hair. "I won't be able to relax, and neither will you, if you're here, knowing that they're running around at the inn dealing with all the holiday madness."

Vic's expression radiated pain, the mental struggle over what he should do showing on his features as his brow creased and the muscles ticked in his clenched jaw. He let out a long sigh.

"All right. I'll agree to that. But promise me you'll rest? And keep my phone with you wherever you go, even if it's in the bathroom. Oh, and I'll be back every hour to check on you. Deal?"

Kellan gave Vic a soft kiss, his poor, stressed-out mate trying so hard. "It's a deal."

CHAPTER ELEVEN

*V*ic paced the kitchen, checking the wall clock then shoving his hands in his pockets as he continued moving from the walk-in cooler to the utility sink then back again.

I promised not to check on him every thirty minutes, to only do it every hour.

Christmas Eve had arrived which was already five days later than when Dr. Arthur had checked Kellan. Five days later than when he'd predicted Kellan would lay the egg at any moment.

Ha! Great doctor he is.

Skip appeared from the dining room. "Last customer's gone, boss man. Dora's locking up now. Shouldn't take too long to finish up in there, the busser has been staying on it and the servers already tipped out." He crossed his arms. "Why don't you go be with your little daddy swan for a while. There's almost three hours to go before the midnight run."

Vic halted. *Shit. Forgot all about that.* "Yeah... I dunno if I'll be going this year."

"Aw, come on. You said you wouldn't miss it."

Vic ran a hand over the top of his head. "I know. But I've never been on the verge of becoming a father before either."

Skip scratched his jaw. "Don't that part happen later, though? He has to pop out that egg first, right? So what if you ain't there for that. It's not like you can help him do it or anything. And you won't even get to see the kid until who knows when. Come on. Hang out with us."

Vic clenched his fists. He wasn't about to treat his mate like that. "Skip, don't piss me off right now. I'm a very stressed out father-to-be and, while I'm glad I'll be missed, making sure Kellan isn't alone or afraid when it's time for him to lay his egg takes precedence over anything else."

Skip held up his hands in surrender. "All right, don't sweat it. I'll tell the gang." He untied then yanked his bib apron over his head. "And tell the kid from me that I hope he has a Merry Christmas." Skip averted his gaze and coughed into his fist. "We've missed him around here."

Vic didn't shock easily, but Skip had just managed to surprise the hell out of him. He didn't know the salty old guy had it in him. "I will, Skip. He'll appreciate it."

Once Vic had verified that everything was taken care of in the restaurant and had wished everyone a Merry Christmas as they went on their way, he wandered over to the panel to shut off the interior lights. He paused, a smile tugging at his lips as his gaze traveled around the room, warmth filling his heart as he admired the myriad of decorations and ornaments that Kellan was in a large part responsible for. With a sigh, he flipped the switches, and section by section, the room darkened.

Vic grabbed his coat of the stand then made his way through the connecting hallway to check in on the night clerk before heading home to Kellan.

"Merry Christmas, Don. Everything okay out here? Need a break before I take off?"

Don glanced up from the magazine he'd been flipping through and smiled. "Merry Christmas to you too. I'm good, Vic. Thanks."

Vic responded with a nod and a wave, anxious to get back to the cabin. He rushed through the chilly night air, an unnamable urgency pushing him to move faster. When he reached the cabin, he fumbled with the key. He'd never bothered with one in the past, but once he'd moved Kellan in, he hadn't been able to stop himself from getting a lock put in.

The moment the door opened, he was surprised by the quiet and that the fire had died down to the point where only embers glowed. His stomach fluttered, his heart seeming to rise into his throat as he quickly shut the door behind him. He didn't want to call out and wake Kellan if he was resting, so he moved swiftly to the bedroom instead.

When he pushed the door to the darkened bedroom open, a sliver of light from the floor lamp in the living room filtered in, casting a pale glow on Kellan's face. He was curled up in the middle of the nest, his hands folded under his chin. All he wore was Vic's robe, the way he'd done all week. He'd refused to put on anything else. Since it appeared as though he was asleep, Vic didn't want to bother him. Right as he turned to leave, Kellan's barely audible voice sounded.

"Vic? What time is it?"

Vic approached the bed then gingerly sat on the edge. Ever since Kellan had built the nest in the middle of the mattress, they hadn't used the large bed to sleep in together. Vic had set up a foam mattress at the other end of the bedroom for them to share. The rest of the time, Kellan would lie in the blanket nest.

"Hi, sweetheart. I just closed the restaurant a little while ago, so it's almost nine-thirty. How are you feeling?" Vic tried to keep his voice casual, even though Kellan's hooded eyes and sluggish movements worried him.

"So... tired. Heavy." He tried to push himself up but fell against the blankets instead.

Vic reached for him, but Kellan pushed his hands away. "My skin is heavy, too. Raw, like my nerves are on fire." He sighed. "It's not you, Vic. I love you more than anything. I just don't want to be touched right now."

"Of course, sweetheart. Whatever you need." *I feel so useless.* "Can I get you some water? Or anything else?"

Kellan licked his lips, his eyelids still drooping. "Yes, thank you. Water would be good."

Vic rushed to get Kellan a drink, tip-toeing around as if any noise at all might disturb him. Once he'd helped support Kellan so he could take a few swallows of water, he gently lowered him back down.

"I'm going to build up the fire again, but I'll be right back. I'm not going anywhere."

"The midnight run..."

Vic hadn't wanted to leave Kellan's side for the run even before he'd begun acting strange. He sure as hell wasn't going anywhere now.

"I already told Skip I couldn't make it and he's passing the message along to everyone else. Oh, and Skip wanted me to tell you Merry Christmas and that he misses you."

Kellan tried to blink his eyes open, but he seemed to give up and they fell closed again. "Skip really said he misses me?"

"Well, in so many words he did. You know how he is."

One corner of Kellan's mouth quirked. "Yeah. I do."

Kellan remained quiet and Vic was at a loss. He didn't want to bother him if he was trying to sleep but he was also frantic to verify that he was okay.

Maybe I should call Dr. Arthur.

Vic found his phone on the nightstand where he'd left it for Kellan, then exited the room as softly as he could. He'd been in

such a hurry to get to his mate, that he hadn't taken off his boots
yet. He pulled the bedroom door almost all the way closed,
leaving it open a crack to have a better chance at hearing Kellan
should he call out.

Once he'd removed his boots and outer layers of clothing, he
put in a call to Dr. Arthur. After six rings, the call went to voicemail and Vic gritted his teeth in frustration. He understood that it
was late on a holiday evening, but dammit, this was about Kellan!
He left a quick 'call me immediately' message then set the phone
on the coffee table so he could build the fire back up.

Every five minutes or so, he'd peek in the bedroom to see if
anything had changed with Kellan. Then he'd poke at the fire,
check his voicemail in case the phone had randomly decided not
to ring, then start the process all over again. At one point, he
decided to make himself a snack, but after two bites of ginger-
bread, he lost interest.

The clock crept closer to midnight and Vic had to admit he
was exhausted. Between the extra long day at the restaurant and
inn, combined with the high levels of stress draining him, he
could barely keep his eyes open. When he went into the bedroom
to get out of his clothes and see if Kellan wanted to join him on
the foam mattress, he was stunned to discover that Kellan had
managed to get himself in a somewhat upright position.

Kellan sat cross-legged in the middle of the blanket nest, his
body curled forward with his chin resting against his chest. He'd
wrapped his arms around himself but still appeared to be asleep.
Vic pondered what to do. Kellan had made it clear he didn't want
Vic touching him at the moment yet being separated from him
entirely was unthinkable. Finally, he came up with a solution.

After he'd changed into a pair of flannel pajamas, something
he hadn't bothered wearing since Kellan had moved in, he
checked to make sure the house was secure and the fire properly
banked. Vic kept his footsteps soft as he moved through the room,

taking one last glance at their Christmas tree with the string of multi-colored twinkling lights.

When he reentered the bedroom, Vic gathered a wool blanket from the foam mattress, then carefully climbed onto the bed with Kellan. He made sure to keep from jostling the blanket nest, settling himself at one edge and curling up on his side. Vic wrapped the blanket around his shoulders, arranging it around his legs the best he could in the awkward position.

Vic gazed up at Kellan. His mate's breathing was slow, but steady, and somewhere deep inside Vic believed that Kellan was doing exactly what he was supposed to be doing. The gods would watch over his beautiful swan and keep their egg safe.

Soon, Vic's eyes grew heavy, but he fought against the sleep trying to take him. *No, not yet. Just a little longer.* He didn't want Kellan to go through the egg-laying all by himself, not when Vic could be there and offer encouragement, to share in the moment and reassure him if he became scared.

The wool blanket was doing its job and Vic had warmed up nicely. His eyelids fluttered, so he tried to keep his focus on Kellan, tried to keep from drifting off.

Kellan. My precious mate, my love...

The song of a cardinal invaded Vic's dream and he tried to ignore it in favor of the imaginary outing he was enjoying with Kellan on the lake during some future summer. *We can bring the baby. I bet it will be a water baby, same as its daddy.* The slow trill of the winter bird cut through Vic's peaceful world and his eyes flew open, his brain registering it was morning right as his eyes adjusted to the light.

He yelped, his arms flailing for a second before he tumbled off the bed and landed with a thump onto the braided rug. Vic lay there for a moment, his heart pounding, trying to work out whether he was still in a dream or truly awake. He sucked in a deep breath, then pushed up from the floor. He peered over the edge of the bed, his eyes widening at the scene before him.

A majestic swan, pure white and breathtakingly beautiful, was perched on the blanket nest, its beak tucked under one wing. Vic smiled, relief flooding him as he realized what had happened.

Kellan.

His mate had shifted. Whatever had been wrong was right again. Christmas morning had brought him the best gift ever. Vic's jaw went slack as the swan gently morphed into Kellan, the feathers seeming to dissolve and the form of the giant bird gradually becoming human. The display fascinated Vic, Kellan's shift not as jarring as what Vic experienced when he changed back and forth with his wolf.

Once Kellan emerged as completely human, Vic gasped at the sight of the perfect, cream-colored egg Kellan had wrapped his body around. Kellan locked gazes with him and smiled.

"I'm okay now, Vic, and so is the egg."

"Oh sweetheart, I'm so happy." He wiggled his fingers, desperate for contact with his mate. "Can I touch you?"

Kellan grinned, his eyes bright and complexion rosy. "And you should kiss me too."

Vic climbed back on the bed and scooted as close to the nest as he dared. He had no idea how fragile the egg might be.

"You can get closer." Kellan kept one arm wrapped protectively around the egg, but lifted the other up in invitation. "You should get used to the egg. I might need you to help once in a while during the incubation period."

Vic moved into Kellan's embrace, careful not to put any pressure against the shell or Kellan. "I'll do whatever I can, but I don't think it's safe for me to sit on that."

Kellan snort-giggled. "No, you would do what I'm doing right now. Cuddle with it, keep it warm. Plus, if we also keep the cabin warm, I can cover it with the blankets for short periods of time and it'll be fine."

Vic caressed the smooth shell that protected his unborn child. "Did that swan shifter Dr. Arthur put you in touch with explain all that?"

"His name is Jonas, and yes he did."

"So, it's okay if I take care of the egg sometimes too? It isn't only the egg-layer who does that?"

"No, not at all."

Kellan snuggled around the egg even more, leaning across the top of it to steal a kiss from Vic. Vic moaned into Kellan's mouth as they deepened the exchange—his mate tasted so damn good. The egg was pressed between them, and the truth of them being a family filled his heart to overflowing. Vic ended the kiss with one final lick across Kellan's bottom lip.

"You must be cold now that you've shifted back." Vic picked up the wool blanket that had flown off him when he'd fallen from the bed. "Here you go." He draped it over Kellan's form. "I'll go stoke the fire and get it roaring again. Do you want something to eat?"

"Yes! I'm starving. I have some juice in there from yesterday, but I'd love a cinnamon roll, too."

More relief flooded Vic. His mate was back to normal. "Good thing I saved you one then, huh?" He winked at Kellan who laughed in response.

Vic placed another kiss on Kellan's forehead then rushed around, getting the fire going and making some fresh juice for Kellan. As he placed the juice, cinnamon roll and some coffee on a tray, the twinkling of the tree lights got his attention.

Hmm.

He brought the tray into the bedroom, then set it on the floor next to the bed. At Kellan's perplexed expression, Vic jerked a thumb over his shoulder. "Hold on, I have to grab one more thing."

Vic scurried to the living room then retrieved the item he wanted. As soon as Kellan's gaze landed on the gift bag holding the stuffed wolf they'd bought at the market, he slapped a hand to his mouth, his eyes glittering, but happy. Vic sat on the bed and placed the bag next to the egg.

"For our baby. I'll always protect and love them as I protect and love you." Vic leaned over and kissed the top of the shell peeking out from under the blankets.

Kellan grabbed Vic's hand, twining their fingers together. "I love you, Vic, my big bad wolf." A lone tear slid down Kellan's cheek, but his smile remained wide. "Merry Christmas."

Vic pressed a kiss to Kellan's palm. "Merry Christmas, sweetheart."

EPILOGUE

Kellan & Vic's New Year's Eve

*V*ic glanced around the restaurant—the crowded room filled with cheery revelers as everyone celebrated New Year's Eve. He narrowed his eyes as he searched the group for Kellan. His mate had told him he'd be right back, but Vic hadn't seen Kellan for a while and had noticed he hadn't been in a party-going mood before they'd walked across the parking lot from the cabin.

"One more blanket, Vic. We need one more blanket."

Since Vic didn't know a thing about nests or incubating eggs, he deferred to Kellan on the subject every time. The only thing in the world as important to him as Kellan was the life growing inside that egg. He'd do whatever it took to protect them both. Once Kellan had added the additional covering, they'd finally headed to the party.

Better late than never.

Deciding he wouldn't be able to relax until he knew where Kellan was, he wound his way through the guests dancing on the cleared-out center of the restaurant to where Dora stood near the front, drinking and laughing with a man he'd never seen before. In some ways, he believed he might be acting too cloying and needy. Kellan was an adult and had the right to go wherever he liked without announcing it or seeking permission.

But once Vic had discovered that Kellan was carrying his egg, he'd been compelled to know where he was at all times. He hoped to hell he wasn't smothering his omega. *But I'm his Alpha. It's my duty to make sure he's protected.* Vic frowned. They were both in new territory. *We should discuss this.* Although, they couldn't do much talking until he found out where Kellan was.

"Hey Dora. Have you seen Kellan?"

Dora giggled as she leaned against her companion. "No, Vic. I've only had eyes on *one* shifter this evening." She gazed up at the rugged, thirtyish man as she looped her arm through his. "Barry and I have been getting reacquainted."

Barry grinned down at her. "Yeah. *Very* reacquainted."

They both dissolved into snickers and snorts and Vic could see he was wasting his time. He was happy that Dora was enjoying herself, but the pull from his mate tugged at him.

Vic cleared his throat. "Okay, thanks. If you'll excuse me?"

With no acknowledgement from the clearly distracted pair, Vic decided to head to the kitchen in case the increasingly raucous gathering had begun to stress Kellan out. *He might be seeking a respite from all this.* Vic had never been much of the loud party type, but the yearly bash he held for his staff and their families was something they looked forward to. He realized that while he wasn't much of a social butterfly, others weren't of the same mindset. Since Kellan held the same attitude, Vic wouldn't be surprised to discover he'd snuck away so he could avoid the madness for a bit. As soon as he found Kellan, he'd suggest they make their goodbyes and go home. Dora had already promised to close up for him anyway.

As he passed the bar, Vic spotted one of his reception clerks,

Mark. *Looks like he's found a date.* Vic had never seen Mark with anyone before, but it appeared as though he was very close to the guy he was kissing and groping. *And who's doing plenty of groping back.* Vic decided he'd bother them for a moment since Kellan had been getting better about trying to be friends with the young witch.

"Um, sorry to interrupt you and…"

A spark of recognition hit him now that he'd gotten closer to the pair in the low lighting. *Right, psychic investigator guy. Huh.*

The smile Mark beamed back at him told Vic more than words ever could. Whatever was going on between the two men wasn't just a party-induced fling.

"Hey, Vic. You remember J.C., right?"

Vic extended his hand to J.C., and once the man had extricated one that had been wrapped around Mark's waist, he accepted and gave Vic's hand a firm shake. "Hi, Vic. Nice to see you again."

"You too, J.C." While he didn't want to be rude, the more minutes that passed without knowing where Kellan was, the more anxious he became. "So, Mark. I was wondering if you'd noticed where Kellan might have gone?"

Mark furrowed his brow, glancing around the restaurant, much as Vic had done earlier. "Actually, I did. He'd offered to see if he could find me some grape juice in the back, but he never returned."

"Oh. That's odd. He's usually very good about things like that." Vic's stomach that had been anxious started twisting even more. "If you guys'll excuse me, I'll go check the kitchen."

"Yeah, sure Vic." Mark grabbed his arm as he began to walk away. "And when you find him, wish Kel a happy New Year for me." Mark released Vic, letting out a small laugh as he did. "And you too, of course."

"Same to you guys."

Vic dipped his chin once then turned to make his way to the kitchen. He understood what Mark's intent had been. Kellan had finally warmed up to him and accepted that witches weren't evil, so Mark had been going out of his way to reinforce the goodwill he'd been building.

Vic pushed his way through the kitchen door and was treated to the sight of Skip chugging a beer while sitting on a crate of apples. Skip straightened, his eyes widening the second he spotted Vic. He shoved the beer bottle behind him.

"Boss man! Party goin' okay? Need more crab puffs?"

Vic sighed. "The crab puff situation seems to be well in hand. How's your transportation situation?"

"My...?" Skip's cheeks reddened. "Oh. Uh, me, Dora and a couple other people have a taxi lined up for later."

Vic nodded. "Good. Why don't you go join the others in the dining room? It'll be easier to monitor the crab puffs from there."

Skip rose from the crate, slowly bringing the beer out from behind his back. "Thanks, boss. Appreciate it."

"One more thing." Vic's eyes darted around the empty room. "Have you seen Kellan?"

Skip drew his eyebrows together. "Yeah. About thirty minutes ago, I think. He was headed out the back door and I assumed he was on his way to your guys' place."

Vic let out a relieved sigh. It all made sense now. "Good, good." He scrubbed his face with one hand. "Then tell Dora I probably won't be back tonight. I'm leaving you two in charge." Vic smirked. "Please don't let everyone tear my restaurant to shreds?"

Skip snorted. "You got it."

After wishing Skip a happy New Year, Vic rushed out the back door, anxious to get to his mate. *And our egg.*

∽

*K*ellan rested his cheek on the top of the egg, closing his eyes as he gently embraced it. He'd already stoked the fire again and had added another blanket to the base of the shell the moment he'd made it to the cabin. All he'd been able to think of the whole time at the restaurant was whether the egg was okay or not. Jonas, the swan shifter Dr. Arthur had put him in touch with, had assured Kellan that as long as the egg was well-covered and the room remained warm, it was okay to leave it for a few hours a day.

But Kellan couldn't bring himself to do such a thing.

For the first few days after Christmas, he'd barely left it to go to the bathroom, let alone anything else. Vic had offered to keep it warm for him so he could have a break now and then, and while that was normal for the mate to help in incubating the egg, Kellan had been too nervous to leave his future hatchling for even a moment. Once Kellan had realized he was not only being unfair to Vic, but that wolves were naturally warmer than swans, he'd relented.

It turned out that Vic was an amazing egg warmer, and Kellan thought he could watch him for hours as he snuggled with their future hatchling, his big, strong body keeping their egg safe. The New Year's party was the first time they'd actually left the egg unattended entirely, and while he knew in his mind that it was fine, understood the logic of keeping the nest warm without either of them present, after an hour he hadn't been able to stand it any longer.

Kellan kissed the top of the egg. *I hope Vic isn't mad at me.*

Right then, the front door clicked open and a *whoosh* of wind breezed in. "Kellan? Are you here?"

Kellan detected the undertone of worry in Vic's voice. "I'm in the bedroom!" He didn't feel the need to add that he was with their egg. He figured Vic had already come to that conclusion on his own.

The sound of shuffling fabric and the clunk of heavy boots on their entryway floor could be heard. A few moments later, Vic entered their bedroom, the one lamp on the nightstand the only light in the room.

Vic smiled as his gaze landed on first him, then their egg. "Hey, sweetheart. I thought I might find you here." His brow creased as he sat gingerly on the edge of the mattress. "Is everything okay?"

"It's fine. I just couldn't help myself. Are you mad at me?"

Vic's features softened. "Of course not. Whatever you need to do to take care of our hatchling-to-be is more important than anything else."

Kellan reached out to Vic, wiggling his fingers until Vic laced them with his own. "You're the best mate ever, Vic. I'm sorry I'm ruining the party for you."

Vic gave their joined hands a squeeze. "Not even close. I'm not a fan of any kind of party, especially loud ones, and I'd rather be here with you anyway." Vic cleared his throat and lowered his head, his nervousness apparent to Kellan.

"What is it, Vic?"

Vic lifted his gaze. "Is it all right that I need to be near *you* so much? I don't want you to feel smothered."

Kellan couldn't believe his ears. He'd been wondering the same thing. "No! I've been trying not to smother *you*."

Vic arched his eyebrows before letting out a snorting chuckle. "Listen to us. We're quite the pair."

Kellan smiled, tugging on Vic's hand. He took the hint and moved closer until he was wrapped around the other side of the egg, the three of them remaining connected as they embraced the egg together while still holding hands.

Something else had been nagging at Kellan, though. While

he knew Vic loved him and was thrilled about the upcoming baby, Kellan had overheard Skip talking to another wolf when he had very first arrived in Vale Valley. Skip had voiced aloud something Kellan had wondered about for a long time. If Vic didn't give Kellan the claiming bite, did that mean they weren't true, fated mates after all?

Vic was lying on his side, with his head propped up in his free hand. "Even though nothing's bothering me, it sure seems as if something's bothering you, sweetheart. This is a night to celebrate the New Year, especially for us." Vic smiled and rubbed his cheek against the creamy shell of the egg. "We're starting a family. Please talk to me, I want you to be happy."

"Oh, but I am! Happier than I could ever imagine I'd be. But..." Why was he being so pushy, so *needy*? Vic had given him everything, had showered him with more love than he'd thought possible. Every day with his mate was wonderful. Why couldn't he just be grateful for that instead of wishing for even more? "I have a question, but I don't want you to think I'm being greedy or unappreciative."

Vic's brow wrinkled again. "I would never think that."

Kellan chewed on his bottom lip. "Um, I know about claiming bites and what they mean for a werewolf. And... Well..."

The light of understanding crossed Vic's features. "Oh. Oh, I see."

Vic sighed and let go of Kellan's hand. Kellan tensed, his stomach dropping, wanting to kick himself for even bringing up the subject. Maybe there were some things he didn't want to know after all.

But instead of moving away, Vic came around to Kellan's side of the bed and wrapped his large frame around him, cocooning him in a warm, comforting embrace. "I didn't bite you because I don't want to change your swan. I'm not entirely sure what would happen, but if I bit a human, they would become a werewolf. I want you exactly how you are."

Kellan angled his body so he could lock eyes with Vic. "But are we still true mates, even if you don't bite me?"

Vic smiled then nuzzled Kellan's head, scenting him and hugging him tighter. "I *know* we are. The claim bite is a statement to the pack that you're mine, all paws off. But..." Vic released Kellan, then encouraged him to turn so they could face each other. "Here's the thing. You know how few of my pack are left. That leaves almost five thousand residents of Vale Valley who my claim bite would have zero impact on."

Vic's eyes glistened in the minimal light. "I was holding off on this because of all the excitement and worry over the egg. However, I don't want you to doubt my true intentions toward you for even one second." Vic clasped his hand again. "Kellan, I love you in a way I hadn't known I was capable of. And I want the whole world to know that truth, as well as sending them a message that they'd better keep their paws, wings, talons, fins—or anything else—off my omega. Kellan, will you do me the honor of marrying me?"

Kellan gasped then choked on a sob as he tried to respond. He couldn't push out even one syllable, so he launched himself into Vic's arms instead. Kellan peppered Vic's face, neck and head with kisses, clutching his amazing and loving wolf. Finally, he pulled himself together long enough to answer his mate.

"Yes, yes, yes! A million times, yes." Kellan framed Vic's cheeks, marveling at his handsome face with the softest, sweetest eyes he'd ever seen, then smashed his lips against Vic's. He broke the connection with a contented sigh. "I love you so much, too. Can we get married tomorrow?"

Vic's eyes widened as his jaw dropped. "I'd marry you right now, sweetheart, but tomorrow's a holiday. We wouldn't be able to get a license. Plus, most of our friends aren't in town or having their own celebrations. Chance and Grayson are getting married tonight, and of course, Mateo and Lance are on their honeymoon."

Kellan slumped. *Vic is right.* But oh, how he wanted to do it right away. "That's true. I have to shop for your ring anyway, and I don't want to leave the egg." He frowned. "And I guess there wouldn't be much of a honeymoon while it's still incubating."

They'd made love only once since he'd laid the egg, and that hadn't been until the day before. While Kellan appreciated how respectful Vic had been by not asking for sex, Kellan hadn't been able to stand it any longer. For his first long break from the egg, he'd taken the opportunity to jump Vic the first chance he'd gotten. Kellan had pushed Vic against the couch cushions and ridden his cock until they'd both screamed out their simultaneous releases. Then, they'd collapsed into each other's arms, dozing off until some mysterious, inner clock had abruptly awoken Kellan and drawn him back to the nest.

Vic brushed Kellan's hair back from his face. "We'll plan something special for later, make it a *real* celebration and invite our closest friends."

Kellan sucked in a sharp breath. "Ooh, I know! Can we have our wedding by the lake in the spring? The baby should be big enough by then and it won't be snowing. I really want to get married by the water." Kellan lowered his chin. *I'm being so self-centered. It's Vic's day too.* "But if there's somewhere else you'd rather..."

Vic placed a gentle kiss on Kellan's lips. "I think by the lake would be perfect."

Kellan grinned up at Vic. "Thank you, Vic. Hey, do you think Skip would be insulted if I asked Sweet Bites to do the catering?"

Vic chuckled. "Unless you want meatloaf and mac and cheese for our wedding reception, I think having the crepes is a great idea. I'm partial to the mushroom chicken one myself."

"Oh my, I like the spinach artichoke and the shrimp and crab one the same. I can't decide."

Vic chuckled. "Then we should have both."

"Awesome. Do you think Chance's band would play at the reception?"

Vic's gaze wandered over Kellan's face as he continued to pet back his hair, the ghost of a smile on his lips. "I think he'd love to, sweetheart."

An explosion of fireworks in the distance and pot banging and cheers from the parking lot jerked him from his wedding-induced trance. Kellan gasped. "Is it midnight?"

Kellan squeaked as Vic yanked him onto his lap and crushed their mouths together. The heated kiss gradually slowed into one filled with soft touches and slow exploration. Vic pressed his forehead to Kellan's.

"Happy New Year, sweetheart."

Kellan smiled, his heart filled to bursting. "Happy New Year, fiancé."

As it had been with Christmas, they shared holiday wishes for the first time. Kellan sent a thank you to the stars, filled with the knowledge that they would exchange those sentiments for many, many years to come.

A HATCHLING FOR VALENTINE'S: A VALENTINE ROMANCE

(Vale Valley Season 2, Book 8)

A Hatchling for Valentine's: A Valentine Romance (Vale Valley Season 2, Book 8)

Copyright ©2019 M.M. Wilde

First Edition

Cover design by Fantasia Frog Designs

Edited by Barham Editorial

Published by Knight Ever After Publishing

All Rights Reserved

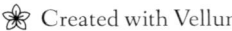 Created with Vellum

Again, I have to give a huge thank you to author Giovanna Reaves for inviting me to be a part of the Vale Valley world that she created. I've grown to love this mysterious, secret town that is a sanctuary to those special beings—whether shifter, magical or from an omegaverse world—who are in need of love and a permanent home. And a special thank you goes out to all the lovely readers who have embraced this fantasy world. You rock!

CHAPTER ONE

*V*ic couldn't keep still. He didn't know how Kellan did it. His dilemma wasn't made any better by the fact that he was terrified he might damage the egg if he made a sudden move or put too much pressure on the shell. This was especially the case since the difference in size between him and Kellan was marked. Although, he had to admit that while Kellan was small, it didn't prevent him from being rather feisty.

As Vic trailed his fingertips from the top of the rounded point of the egg to the swell of the hard, creamy surface where it was nestled in a jumble of soft blankets and towels, he marveled at how abruptly his life had changed in only a few months. He'd gone from being a lonely Alpha wolf who had despaired of ever finding any mate, to falling madly in love with a sweet and salty swan omega who also happened to be his *fated* mate.

And now we're starting a family.

First their hatchling would be born then they would be married next to Vale Lake in the spring. Vic sighed and placed a gentle kiss on the egg he had his body loosely wrapped around.

He'd been truly blessed by the gods after losing his pack and being alone for so many years.

Right as Vic was about to doze off to thoughts of the new house he'd decided he wanted to build for his growing family, he was jostled awake by the sound of his mate's voice booming in the living room.

"Vic! Wait till you see what I got!"

Vic chuckled to himself. He'd given Kellan a credit card of his own and told him to go out and buy whatever they needed for the baby. It wasn't as if they had months before the baby hatched. Swan shifter babies arrived much sooner than wolf shifter babies did. Vic reflexively petted the egg, an uneasy twinge in his gut nagging at him.

Dr. Arthur will be by soon. Maybe he has some new insights.

They had yet to find anyone who had experienced the birth of a part swan, part wolf shifter baby. Other than not moving the egg, keeping it warm and allowing it to hatch naturally, everything else would be a whole lot of guessing mixed in with a generous portion of surprise.

"Look!" Kellan burst into the room with a large plastic bag from the local department store where many of the residents shopped. Whatever it contained was about a quarter of the size of Kellan and housed in a box. He gave Vic a messy kiss on his lips before excitedly continuing. "Remember how I saw that homemade baby food recipe channel online? Well, I found this amazing food processor on sale!" Kellan grinned as he set the bag on the edge of the bed then peeled it down to show off his purchase. "See? They even had it in red."

Vic sat up enough to get a good look at the box so he could read all the features. "Wow. This *is* a nice model for the house." He smiled at Kellan. "So is the red." Vic plucked at his beard as he considered whether he wanted to ask the next question. "What do swan shifter babies eat?"

Kellan chewed on his lower lip. "You might not want to know. But it'll be pureed, so it shouldn't bother you *too* much. That show I saw has lots of fruit and vegetable recipes too, so I can just mix the—"

Vic held up his hand. "That's okay. You're right. Don't want to know."

Kellan's cheeks flushed. "I'll just take this to the kitchen then."

"Hey." Vic gestured for him to move closer. "How about another kiss first?"

With an even bigger grin, Kellan leaned down and opened up to Vic, an invitation for more than a quick peck. Vic cupped Kellan's cheek, stroking his face with his thumb while moving his tongue through Kellan's mouth, tasting the man he ached for every minute of the day. He drew back but held Kellan's gaze.

"Did you get any swimming in?"

The day was sunny for a change, and Kellan had so few opportunities to be away from the egg. It had already been a few weeks since he'd laid it and the snowy weather hadn't let up.

"I did. I shifted and paddled around for a while." Kellan straightened as his expression fell.

Vic furrowed his brow. "What? Didn't you enjoy it?"

"I'm... I'm not complaining, I swear. It's just that there aren't any other swans to swim with. Not even geese or ducks." He smirked. "Well, not ones that can shift, anyway. I'm not used to being the lone water fowl. It's unnatural."

Vic reached out and clasped Kellan's hand. "I'm sorry, sweetheart. Maybe some will move to Vale Valley soon."

Kellan gave a small nod. "Yeah. I suppose." He laced his fingers with Vic's. "What about you? You never did the midnight run on Christmas Eve and you haven't done anything like that since."

Vic couldn't deny he'd been itching to get out for a good

night's romp but hadn't felt right leaving Kellan alone with the egg. His concern was silly in some ways. What was likely to happen? He had to admit that his almost rabid need to watch over Kellan and his unhatched child had caught him off-guard.

"I'll see what Skip and the other guys are up to this week. Now that there seems to be a break in the storms, maybe we can pull something together."

A smile lit up Kellan's face. "That sounds awesome. I don't want me and the baby to mess up your life."

Vic gasped, sitting up with a start. He yanked Kellan to him until he stumbled onto his lap then wrapped his arms around him in a firm embrace. "Don't *ever* say that and please don't think it. I was only marking time before you came along. *Nothing* makes me happier than having you and having a baby on the way. Do you realize how long I was alone, how I'd given up on ever finding a mate?"

Kellan relaxed in Vic's hold and lay his head against his chest. "I know, I do. I guess letting go of all the ugly words my brother Finn and the others always drilled into me isn't as easy as I'd thought. Over and over for years about how useless and in the way I was." Kellan peered up at him. "I'll get better, I promise."

Vic sighed then cupped the back of Kellan's neck, pressing his lips to Kellan's forehead. "You're fine exactly how you are. I wish I could make that little shit pay for the way he treated you. No matter what, though, I adore and love you and I want this baby more than I've ever wanted anything. *That* is one fact you can be certain of."

At last Kellan's smile was back and his eyes bright and filled with joy the way Vic hoped they would always be.

"You're the best mate ever, Vic. Thanks."

A tickle in Vic's nose and a burning in his eyes brought home the truth of how much Kellan and the baby really meant to him.

And I'll kill anyone who dares hurt either one of them.

~

*K*ellan had put away his food processor and other purchases, then called in his and Vic's dinner order to the restaurant. Once he'd taken over the nesting duties, Vic had headed across the parking lot to grab their food. One catfish for him and some prime rib for Vic later, they were on their sides playing cards on the bed, the egg perched between them on the pile of soft towels and blankets he'd constructed over a month before when he'd gone into his pre-egg-laying frenzy. He snorted to himself. What a shock that had been.

Vic lifted an eyebrow. "You up to something sneaky with those cards over there?"

Kellan shook his head. "Just remembering." A bit of guilt coursed through him. "Do you think Dora and the others who came to visit are still mad?"

Vic sighed. "Sweetheart, they were never mad at you to begin with. And now that your swan knows they're safe to be around the egg, they can come back and visit again another time."

Kellan's lip trembled. "I didn't mean to bruise Dora's face." The restaurant's hostess was his closest friend and she'd helped him so much when he'd first arrived in Vale and begun working as a server. "She ran out of here crying and I just... I just..." He caught a sob in his throat, tossing down his cards on the comforter as tears filled his eyes. "I don't understand why I did that!"

Vic rose from the bed and came around the end to sit next to him. He petted Kellan's hair back from his forehead.

"Did you discuss what happened with Jonas?"

The swan shifter who lived in the same town as Dr. Arthur, and who the doctor had put him in touch with, had helped him with so many of his questions. Kellan picked at the bed covering, unable to hold Vic's gaze. "I was too embarrassed."

"But, he's there for you as a resource and you told me he's helped you with so many other questions."

Frustration bubbled up in Kellan. "Why did I have to be raised by a hateful bastard who never told me anything of what to expect!"

Vic grasped his chin and encouraged him to look up. "Hey. Listen to me. I doubt that little shit knew anything either. Doesn't excuse his behavior, but we move forward from here. We don't have to worry about him anymore, right?"

The heaviness in Kellan's heart lifted. Vic always made everything better. "You're right. We don't."

Vic offered him a wide smile. "And Dr. Arthur will be here any minute and you can ask him, okay?"

Kellan nodded. "Okay, I will."

They went back to playing cards while they waited for Dr. Arthur to show up. He'd texted to say he was running late since he was helping his nephew, the new Vale Valley fire chief, to move.

Kellan perused his cards. "Do you have any fours?"

"Go fish."

A knock sounded at the door and Kellan dropped his cards in excitement. Vic chuckled.

"I guess that takes care of that."

Kellan glanced down to see his cards strewn about, face up. "Oh." He shrugged. "That's all right, I was getting bored anyway. We should mess around after he leaves."

Vic snort-chuckled as he rose from the bed. He winked at Kellan. "Much less boring than cards."

Kellan had been horny ever since he'd gotten out of the lake but knew Dr. Arthur would be stopping by, so he hadn't acted on his urge. However, once the avian fertility specialist was gone, he'd heat up the cabin and get Vic naked.

While Vic let Dr. Arthur in, Kellan gathered up the cards

and put them away. The cabin was probably warm enough that they could've put blankets over the egg and played in the other room, but they'd automatically stayed on the bed. There seemed to be some sort of unspoken instinct in play when it came to the nest. They got as much satisfaction out of staying with it as they did out of almost any other activity they shared.

Kellan snickered. *Except for what we'll be sharing later.* Finn and the other guys had never let on how great sex was, so he'd had no idea what to expect. *That's because they probably aren't getting any.* He snickered again.

"Good evening, Kellan. How are you feeling?"

Dr. Arthur entered the bedroom with Vic trailing behind.

"I'm doing great. Is your nephew all moved into his new place?" Kellan was super curious about Avi because he was an eagle shifter.

"Oh yes, we brought the last of the boxes and his clothes tonight." Dr. Arthur rolled his eyes. "We're both glad that's over with."

Dr. Arthur sat on the edge of the mattress and gestured to the egg. Ever since Kellan had almost scratched the doctor's eyes out trying to protect his hatchling, Dr. Arthur always asked first. Kellan nodded.

"That's good." Even though Kellan didn't mind Dr. Arthur examining the egg, it didn't mean he wasn't going to keep a close watch on the proceedings.

Vic peered over the doctor's shoulder. "Can I get you anything to drink?" He might have been asking Dr. Arthur the question, but Vic hadn't taken his eyes off the egg either.

"Oh no, I'm fine." Dr. Arthur pulled his stethoscope from his pocket then proceeded to place the disc on various spots around the egg. "Notice any changes? Movement? Color? Any areas seem to be thinning instead of hardening?"

Kellan swallowed hard. What did it all mean? He hated that

no one had been around to prepare him for this journey. "I haven't noticed anything like that, just that it's stretching and a bit larger since the last time you came."

Dr. Arthur's brow wrinkled, and he pulled a strange metal instrument from his bag. The gadget was metal and could be adjusted so the arms embraced the egg at the base, the middle and the top. He then measured it vertically.

"Hmm, interesting."

Kellan swallowed hard. "Wh-what do you mean?"

Dr. Arthur folded up the measuring tool with a reassuring smile. "Your egg has definitely grown, and the soft patches have almost completely hardened. You're getting closer to the hatch date, whenever that will be." He chuckled. "But I must confess, this baby is going to be much larger than most cygnets."

Kellan and Vic exchanged nervous glances and Vic cleared his throat before addressing Dr. Arthur.

"I suppose that's my fault."

Dr. Arthur angled his body toward Vic then patted his arm. "Now, now. Don't you worry. We've always known things weren't going to follow the typical swan path to hatching. But the egg looks solid, the shell healthy and the baby's heartbeat is strong and steady." Dr. Arthur took the stethoscope from his ears. "You've clearly done a fine job of nesting."

Kellan shifted on the bed, still not entirely reassured. "Should our baby have been moving by now?"

Dr. Arthur rubbed his chin. "Well... yes, under normal circumstances. At three weeks the baby should be large enough that when they shift positions, there would be noticeable movement. But as I said, these *aren't* normal circumstances. I've never attended to a part wolf egg before."

Tears sprung to Kellan's eyes. He'd never thought about it quite that way. "But if Vic fertilized the egg, then shouldn't that mean...?"

Dr. Arthur squeezed Kellan's hand. "I would say that the fact you both are fated mates and he was able to fertilize your egg is a very good sign. Kellan, there've been so many mixed shifter babies, I really don't think you should get overly concerned. I'll keep checking in once a week, but if anything—no matter how slight—changes, please contact me right away." He rose then faced Vic. "My wife and I will be here quite a bit to visit Avi until he gets acclimated to his new home. Rosemary has been kind enough to throw a dinner party in his honor, so we'll be here on the weekend for that. Matter of fact, I'm going to the inn to reserve a room for me and the wife as soon as I leave here."

Vic nodded. "Sounds great, doc. We appreciate you keeping such a close watch on the egg."

"Of course, any time. Once your hatchling arrives, though, you'll want to have him or her checked out at Vale General."

While Vic escorted Dr. Arthur out, Kellan cuddled up to the egg again, caressing it and rubbing his cheek against the shell. Maybe he'd have some alone time with Vic later. For now, he didn't want to leave his nest for even one minute.

CHAPTER TWO

*K*ellan checked the ingredients for the elderberry cobbler he was making for Vic. The confection would go along with the brisket he already had in the oven and the green bean casserole that Skip, the restaurant's chef, had shown him how to make. He wasn't so sure about the goopy mushroom soup that came from a can, but Skip swore by it. Vic had eaten a pile of it at Thanksgiving. Kellan hadn't felt as adventurous, so he'd downed two large bowls of cranberry sauce instead.

After setting everything he needed for the dessert to one side, he double-checked the temperature in the cabin.

Ninety degrees. Perfect.

Despite wanting to spend every waking minute on his nest, it wasn't necessary—especially now that the soft patches allowing for growth were almost all hardened. He and Vic would have six hours to be together, as long as the cabin remained hot and the egg was covered with blankets. One important thing he *had* learned from Jonas, the swan shifter Dr. Arthur had put him in touch with, was that nesting wasn't only about keeping the egg warm—it was about bonding with their unborn child.

Kellan smiled to himself. He could tell it had made a difference in Vic. He'd never let on, but he would peek at Vic and their egg when his mate would take over the nesting duties, would watch him with their egg. Kellan still needed to learn more about Alpha wolves and what their behavior was like toward their young, but Vic was so sweet and loving with the egg, talking to their unborn child through the shell when he thought he was alone. If he'd thought his heart was full of love for his mate before, the sight of him with their hatchling-to-be had cemented his feelings.

The door swung wide and a cold blast of air followed Vic inside. He shook snowflakes out of his hair and beard, stamping his boots on the mat in the entryway to get rid of the powdery residue that still clung to his footwear. Kellan rushed over to greet him.

"Oh no, did the snow cut your run short?"

The storm hadn't been expected until much later. Kellan took Vic's jacket from him to hang on the coat rack while Vic bent down to unlace his boots. He straightened, then toed them off, holding an arm out in invitation to Kellan.

"Nah. Skip had a date with a bear shifter and I wanted to get home to you." He gave Kellan a kiss on the head as he embraced him. "And a little snow won't stop wolves from running, trust me. It's when it turns into a blizzard that it gets a bit dicey." He gave Kellan a squeeze. "The night I found you lost in the woods I hadn't planned to stay out very long. I knew it was gonna be a doozy." Vic angled back to frame Kellan's face with his palms. "I'm so grateful I didn't change my mind about going out that night."

Vic descended on Kellan's lips, moving his mouth over them

in a soft affirmation of his words. Kellan was grateful too. He would've been a goner if Vic hadn't found him when he had.

More confirmation that fate was on our side.

Vic released him then stuck his nose in the air, sniffing. "That smells amazing." He regarded Kellan. "Red meat. Did you need me to get you any fish? Or..." He pursed his lips in what seemed to be an unsuccessful attempt at hiding his disgust. "A frog... or other pond creature? I didn't see any in the fridge."

Kellan giggled at Vic's expression. "No, I'm fine for tonight. I'm having yams and green beans. Plus, I'm making an elderberry cobbler for dessert, so I'll have lots of that." He'd set aside some extra beans for himself so he could eat them sans goop.

Kellan wrapped his fingers around Vic's hand and led him across the living room toward the open kitchen of their small, pine wood cabin. "Will you tell me about your run while I cook? I want to hear some wolfy things."

Vic snorted as he followed behind Kellan. "Wolfy things?"

"Yeah." Kellan dropped Vic's hand to go back to his task. "I want to know more about you, about wolf packs and how all that works." He glanced over his shoulder as he opened the bag of flour. "Plus, our baby will be half wolf, and I should be aware of what they need, what they're like."

Vic tugged at his beard. "Hmm. I guess I hadn't thought too much about that. I mean, I know the baby will be part of me, but..." His eyes darted to the bedroom where their egg rested in the nest. "I guess I always think of them being mostly swan because of the egg and all."

Kellan chewed his lower lip, setting the measuring cup down so he could face Vic. "Does it bother you? I mean, if that happened?"

Vic shook his head. "Gods, no. Even if the baby was all swan, I would still be over the moon." His expression softened as he smiled. "I love you with all my heart, love your swan. How could it ever bother me to have a beautiful child just like his beautiful father?"

A sense of peace washed over Kellan. He might not have had love growing up, but he now had more than he'd ever hoped for. For the rest of his life, he'd be part of a *real* family.

~

*V*ic hadn't missed how antsy Kellan had been all through dinner. He'd also noted the candles from his buddy Grayson's aromatherapy shop which had been lit and placed decoratively around the room. If Kellan was thinking what *he* was thinking, then Vic was up for it as well.

Literally.

They'd both been so focused on the egg that making love and being alone together had no longer been a priority. Vic would never complain or pressure Kellan for sex, but if Kellan was missing their intimacy as much as he was, he wouldn't discourage him either.

Vic had insisted on washing the dishes since Kellan had whipped up such an amazing meal, and Kellan hadn't hesitated to take him up on his offer. He'd then disappeared into the bedroom, which gave Vic even more proof that Kellan was plotting something. In addition, the cabin was hot as fuck, which told him something very important—Kellan didn't intend to nest again right away.

"Vic?"

He turned around and almost dropped the glass he'd been drying. His stunning swan was naked, hard and leaning against the doorframe of the bedroom. He held a bottle in his hand and a towel was draped over his arm.

Vic gave a low whistle. "Damn, sweetheart. You are the most

gorgeous thing I've ever seen. I hope this means what I think it does."

"You won't be disappointed in me if I don't go back on the nest right away?"

Vic frowned. "Is that what you think?" He set down the glass on the counter then beckoned Kellan to him as he moved closer to his mate. "Come here, I want to hold you, touch your soft skin." Once Kellan was secure in his embrace, Vic stroked his back. "Do I make you feel that way? That I think you should be on the nest night and day or else you're not a good father?"

"No, you don't."

Kellan rubbed his cheek against Vic's shirtless chest. There was only so much heat an already hot-blooded wolf could take, so he'd gradually stripped down over the course of their dinner until all he was left wearing were his boxer shorts.

"Then what is it?"

"Well, I'm still so young and you're so responsible and have more experience than me. I was afraid you might think I wasn't mature enough to handle being a daddy."

Vic hugged Kellan close. "Nothing could be further from the truth, sweetheart. I can already tell what an amazing father you'll be." Vic clasped Kellan's shoulders then gazed down at him. "Why, you even tried to peck the eyes out of the doctor. I sure as hell didn't go that far to protect our hatchling."

Kellan gazed up at him. "You promise you're not just saying that?"

Vic smiled, his voice dipping lower as his own arousal took over. "Promise." Unable to hold back any longer, Vic captured Kellan's mouth in a heated kiss, pushing past the seam of his lips, thrusting deeper with each swipe of his tongue. He wanted Kellan in every way possible.

Kellan squeaked into his mouth as he scooped him into his arms and carried him to the sofa. He gently laid Kellan on his back, never breaking the kiss as he continued to plunder his mouth with all the longing and hunger he'd been holding inside for weeks. Breathless, Vic broke the connection so they could draw air and he could get rid of his last vestige of clothing.

As he removed his boxers, his cock sprang free and he didn't miss the way Kellan's tongue darted out, licking his bottom lip before disappearing again. Vic groaned, anxious to experience that wet heat on his hard flesh, to take his pleasure in Kellan's willing mouth.

But what he desired more than anything was to sink his thick cock into the tight ass of his sexy omega and knot him, hold him close while he pumped his seed into his body, his mate unable to break free as they joined together as if they were one.

Vic's gaze traveled from the delectable sight of a nude Kellan to the bottle and towels that had tumbled to the floor next to the couch.

"What's that?"

"The other day when you were on the nest and I went out, I stopped by Creatures of Comfort to pick up some massage oil. Grayson's even got it in special aromatherapy blends now."

Kellan scraped his teeth over his bottom lip and Vic groaned again. *He's trying to drive me crazy.*

Vic cleared his throat. "That so? Which blend is that one?" He pointed to the fallen container.

"Wild musk."

Oh gods. "We'd better give it a try then."

Kellan propped himself up on his elbows. "You want me to rub your back? What about your feet? I bet they're sore after all that running."

Vic shook his head. "No. I want to lick your sweet skin then pour the oil on your body, feel the silk of your flesh as my fingers slide over it."

Kellan's eyes rounded. "Oh my. Okay."

Vic crouched down and scooped up the bottle. He understood the reason for the towels—Kellan had been concerned about staining the couch. Personally, Vic didn't give a shit. He had more important things on his mind.

Kellan reached for the green terrycloth and Vic pushed his hand away. "Lie back and let me take care of you. Let me worry about things tonight. You relax and enjoy."

With a soft push to Kellan's shoulder, Vic was able to get him to obey. He sat on the edge of the couch next to Kellan's thighs then snicked the bottle cap open. The scent of the oil hit his nostrils and his cock throbbed even more. Whatever Grayson had put into his concoction had somehow made him even hotter for Kellan than he already was. He hadn't known such a thing was possible.

Vic's feral wolf spirit rose to the surface and he growled hungrily as he gazed on the lithe body of his mate, the man he wanted in his life forever and ever. With one hand wrapped around the bottle, Vic used the other to cradle Kellan's head, kissing him over and over, tilting his head with each plunge to get as much of Kellan's addicting taste as he could.

"I love you, sweetheart. You're mine, *only* mine."

Kellan smiled, a dreamy expression dancing across his features. "You're only mine too."

Vic nipped at Kellan's chin then licked his way along his jaw until he reached his ear where he nibbled on the lobe. "Agreed. We belong only to each other." Vic latched on to Kellan's throat, sucking and licking, pulling blood to the surface to leave a mark. Until they were married, he didn't want anyone to doubt that Kellan was *his* and no one else's.

Vic drew back to admire his handiwork. The mark was lurid, would deepen to a magnificent scarlet at the base of his mate's throat where it wouldn't be missed by anyone. He continued to lick his way down Kellan's chest, torturing each nipple with love bites, pulling the pebbled nubs with his teeth then soothing them with his tongue as Kellan moaned and writhed beneath him.

He continued the erotic torture until he reached the soft nest of blond curls surrounding Kellan's twitching shaft. Pre-cum leaked from his mate's slit, tiny beads of sticky dew that Vic lapped up with his tongue.

"Vic, oh..."

Kellan thrashed his head from side to side, clutching his fingers in Vic's hair as he circled his hips in seeming desperation. Vic took him out of his misery by swallowing him down in one move, working the muscles of his throat around Kellan's cockhead. Vic sucked and pulled, willed Kellan to give up his seed, to fill Vic's mouth with the wondrous taste of his essence.

"I'm gonna... Vic!"

With a shout, Kellan pulsed warm jets of cum and Vic greedily drank it all. He slowed his movements, gentling his licks so as not to overstimulate him. Vic nuzzled Kellan's groin, pressing his nose in the crease where Kellan's hip joined his pelvis, scented his balls then captured one more drop of seed left uncollected.

Vic straightened and almost dropped the bottle of massage oil he'd completely forgotten about in his lust-driven haze. He locked eyes with Kellan.

"I still want you. Want inside."

Kellan gave a jerky nod. "Yes. That."

Vic set the container down on the rug then wrapped an arm around Kellan's waist, hoisting him up then turning him over. In what seemed like an instinctual response, Kellan thrust his ass in the air. Vic took the invitation. He parted Kellan's cheeks, snaking his tongue up his crease so he could taste every part of him. Never had he been so captivated by a man. For so long, he'd told himself he'd never find his fated mate, so he'd given up on searching for anything beyond a quick release with a lover. But now that he had the one who was meant for him in his arms, he'd never take Kellan for granted.

I'll give him whatever he desires.

Vic prodded at Kellan's tight opening, determined to force his way past the rim guarding his hole. Vic teased Kellan with the tip of his tongue until he had him wriggling and begging for more. What else could Vic do but give it to him?

With an insistent push, Vic breached him, tongue-fucking Kellan's ass with abandon. His own cock was in agony, his balls pulling up in their sac as he fought to keep from coming before Kellan's inner heat was wrapped around his dick. Reluctantly, Vic removed his tongue, desperate to bury himself in Kellan's ass.

Vic eyed the bottle he'd set down. Kellan was already slick, but he still yearned to feel their skin slide together, slippery from the oil. After flipping the cap open again, Vic poured a generous amount into the palm of his hand. He set the bottle aside then rubbed his hands together, coating them with the fragrant substance.

"Love you. Relax and let yourself go."

Vic ran his hands up Kellan's back then gripped his shoulders, gently squeezing and kneading them before repeating the move. After a couple minutes, Vic poured more oil out and continued to massage Kellan, only this time, he rubbed it on his butt cheeks and down his thighs. They would glide with ease against each other as they fucked.

Once he'd coated his lover in a liberal measure of oil, he straddled him from behind then placed his tip against Kellan's willing entrance. Kellan pushed back as if trying to take him in and Vic pressed into him, careful not to breach him too quickly. It took all his willpower to hold himself back from ramming into his mate and possibly hurting him.

A sigh fell from Vic's lips as he filled Kellan's passage, as the grip of Kellan's snug ass encased his cock. He hissed as Kellan squeezed him from the inside. His mate had been innocent when they'd first met, but he'd soon learned what pleased Vic.

Just as Vic had hoped, the sensation of their skin as they slid together created such a delicious friction, he knew he wouldn't last. Kellan gripped him from the inside again, clenching and releasing around his dick and Vic tumbled over the edge, shouting his release as he shot his seed into Kellan. His wolf howled inside as his cock swelled at the base, knotting Kellan to him.

Vic had never given Kellan the claim bite out of worry that he would somehow be changing his swan mate, that Kellan would no longer be the marvelous, amazing man he was. But his wolf wouldn't allow him to resist the urge any longer. Kellan was his rightful, fated mate. He was meant to be claimed by Vic. Nothing about that truth could be wrong.

Throwing his head back and letting loose a throaty howl, Vic then clamped on the crook of Kellan's neck, sinking his teeth into his mate's flesh in a bite he'd never believed he'd have the joy to give. A startled cry burst from Kellan and he struggled for a moment before going limp. Vic's fangs retracted but his knot remained firm. He licked and soothed the bite marks, helping them to heal, yet knowing the scars of his claim would remain as a sign to all that Kellan belonged to him.

Vic wrapped his arm loosely around Kellan's throat as his knot receded. He nuzzled behind Kellan's ear, placing light kisses along his jaw and the back of his neck.

"Did I hurt you too much?"

Kellan clasped the arm Vic had curled around him. "It was sharp, but over with right away. Was that the claiming bite?"

"Yes." He scented Kellan, never able to get enough of his smell. "My wolf drove me on. I hope you're not angry with me."

"Not angry. I'm surprised, but more than anything, so relieved."

Vic jerked up his head. That wasn't at all what he'd expected Kellan to say. "Relieved? I don't understand."

"When you told me you hadn't bitten me because you didn't want to change my swan, I thought maybe it was an excuse. But now I know. You want me as your forever mate."

Vic dropped his forehead to Kellan's shoulders. "Oh, sweetheart. When I proposed, I meant *that* to be how I'd show you I wanted you as my forever mate."

"I'm sorry. I didn't mean to doubt you. I get scared, that's all."

Vic peppered Kellan's neck and shoulders with kisses, then nipped his ear before whispering, "You never have to be scared again. You're stuck with me for good."

Kellan giggled and all was right again with the world.

CHAPTER THREE

*T*he week had gone by without much in the way of changes to the egg, other than the soft patches almost completely hardening. Only a few small areas remained at the base, and Vic wasn't sure what any of it meant. He'd searched online to learn more about swans, but Kellan had caught him and immediately gotten worried that Vic knew something bad about the egg but been afraid to tell him. That had led to a discussion regarding them always being honest with each other no matter what. They'd both agreed never to hide anything, regardless of how frightening the subject was.

However, his search hadn't been very helpful anyway. As it was with wolves and other shifters, the rules weren't always the same as they were with the animal or bird. When he'd finally broken down and called Dr. Arthur, he'd reminded Vic of that and scolded him for looking on the Net rather than calling him with his concerns. He'd also thought to ask another valuable question.

Vic rose from the couch where he'd been relaxing. After

pulling a twelve-hour shift at the Inn and restaurant the day before, he'd vowed to do nothing except lie around and peruse some cabin designs on his tablet. He loved the style of his wood home with the pine and river rock fireplace, but they needed more room.

Especially if our family continues to grow.

Dr. Arthur had already warned them that Kellan's next clutch the following year would likely produce more than one egg. They still hadn't discussed how many kids they wanted or how soon, but Vic hoped Kellan would want a large family. First, they had to make sure that the egg Kellan's swan was incubating in the next room would be all right.

Vic ambled into the kitchen, starting another pot of coffee for Dora and Skip's visit. When he'd spoken to the doc, he'd reassured him that Kellan's swan only went on the attack if it didn't recognize the visitor. Once his swan had been introduced to the person when in the vicinity of the nest and been reassured they meant no harm to the egg, any subsequent visits would be safe.

Vic turned on the coffee machine and it gurgled to life. *I sure as hell hope so.* Kellan already felt so bad over Dora's bruised cheek that his wing joint had caused.

A knock sounded and Vic tensed. "I'll be there in a sec!"

Rustling noises along with some flapping could be heard from the bedroom and he rushed to reassure Kellan's swan. By the time he'd rushed through the door, the white, regal bird had hopped from the bed with his wings held aloft and spread wide. He stuck his beak in the air and let out a loud squealing cry.

Vid raised his, palms out. "Hey, it's okay. That's Dora and Skip at the door, they're our friends. Remember?"

Kellan stretched out his wings once more then settled to his normal swan height. Vic smiled as his mate completed the gentle shift that he never tired of watching. First, Kellan's wings would seem to melt away as his neck shortened. Then the beak and webbed feet would be next while the feathers gradually disappeared. Eventually, a naked Kellan would emerge with his legs and feet tucked under him, hunched over with his head bowed and his arms wrapped around himself.

Vic extended his hand to help his mate to his feet, then guided him to the edge of the bed so he could sit down for a moment while he recovered from his shift. Kellan explained that ever since he'd been carrying the egg, it took him longer to get all his strength back after a shift.

"Do you want the robe?"

Vic plucked the white, terry cloth robe off the mattress he'd dragged into the bedroom to use, since the egg took up the space in the middle of their usual bed. Kellan nodded and accepted the white garment. Technically, it was Vic's, but Kellan had snagged it and made it his own—despite how large and too long it was for him. Vic guessed it was a comfort thing.

"Okay, I'm going to go let our visitors in." He stroked Kellan's cheek. "You come out when you're ready. I made some coffee, so I can keep us busy with that for a minute."

Kellan gave him a sleepy smile. "Thanks, Vic. I won't be too long."

"Take as long as you want." Vic kissed Kellan's forehead, then left the bedroom—closing the door behind him—so he could let their friends in from the cold. He jogged to the front of the cabin to greet them both. "Hey Dora, Skip. Sorry about the delay." Vic gestured for them to come in. "I wanted to make sure Kellan's swan wasn't going to be upset."

Dora touched the fading bruise on her cheek. "I don't have a problem with that." She glanced around the room as if checking for hidden attack swans. "I take it we're safe?"

"He's fine, and honestly, very worried that you're still mad at him."

Dora's brow wrinkled. "Oh man. I don't want him to feel bad. He can't help it." She narrowed her eyes. "Can he?"

Vic snorted. "No, he can't. I spoke to the avian specialist and he explained that now that Kellan's swan is familiar with you both, everything should be fine."

Skip scented the air. "Is that fresh coffee?"

"Yeah, just made it." Vic welcomed the change of subject. "Why don't you guys have a seat while I grab you each a cup."

He'd barely had the chance to head to the kitchen when he about jumped out of his skin.

"*Vic!* Vic, hurry! It *moved!*"

"Holy shit."

Vic almost tripped over his own feet in his haste. He shoved the door open, bursting into the room, his forward momentum nearly sending him crashing to the floor as he attempted to keep from landing on the bed. He grabbed hold of the door knob in the nick of time.

Kellan was perched on the mattress, on his knees with his hands covering his mouth as he gaped at the egg. Dora and Skip rushed in too, although Dora made sure to stay behind Skip, peering over his shoulder at the scene.

"I-is every...everything okay?" Vic could barely push out his words he was so out of breath. *And dizzy.*

Kellan staring up at him with wide eyes. "I think so. I mean, that's good, right?" He grinned. "Maybe that means our baby is about to hatch!"

"Holy shit." Vic bent over and placed his hands on his knees.

Dora cleared her throat. "You said that already."

Vic straightened as he took a deep breath then swiped his hand across his sweaty forehead. "It's so *hot* in here."

Skip grunted. "I was gonna mention that. How can you stand it?"

Vic shot Skip a glare. "The heat is for my *baby*, not your comfort."

"Hmmph." Skip crossed his arms. "Just making an observation. Sheesh."

Vic sighed, wiping his forehead again. "Sorry for snapping at you like that... I'm just..."

He regarded Kellan again who was scooting to the end of the bed on his knees. He tugged at the sleeve of Vic's flannel shirt.

"Should we call Dr. Arthur and ask him?"

"Yeah, definitely." He turned to Dora. "Can you stay with him for a sec while I make the call? Reception is better in the living room."

"Of course." She smiled at Kellan. "As long as he doesn't mind."

Kellan hung his head. "I don't mind." He peered up at her. "I'm sorry about your cheek. I swear I didn't mean it."

"I know, hon. Let's not worry about that anymore, all right?"

Kellan's expression brightened again. "All right." He patted the comforter. "Have a seat. You can touch the egg if you want, but real soft, okay?"

She nodded. "As long as you're sure."

As she reached the side of the bed Kellan was on, he clasped her hand and pulled her closer. Vic wanted to stay and watch, but his nerves had him so jumpy.

"Uh, Kellan. I'm going to make the call now and I'll need to explain things to Dr. Arthur. Did it move a lot, more than once?" Vic eyed the egg. *I wish I could've been here when it happened.* "Has it moved again?"

Kellan continued to stare at their unhatched child as he shook his head. "Not since it moved the one time." He glanced up. "It was sorta like a quick jerk to one side, that's it. But it was *very* noticeable."

Vic's hand shook as he ran it across his head. "Cool, that's good. I'll let him know, see what he says."

Get hold of yourself, dude. He couldn't discern how much of his reaction was terror and how much was excitement.

He left Kellan with their two friends and made his way to the living room. He wanted the baby to be born soon, wanted to see his child, to hold them—but what if something went wrong? No one seemed to have very definitive answers about anything—not even the doctor.

As Vic waited for Dr. Arthur to answer his phone, he sent out a silent prayer to the universe that the doctor would be in town with his nephew instead of his home, which was a few hours away.

"This is Dr. Arthur."

"Doctor! Oh, thank God."

"Is the egg hatching?" His voice was as calm as if he were asking what time it was.

How can he be so blasé about this? "We're not sure. It just moved."

"And?"

Vic frowned at the phone. "What do you mean 'and'? Isn't that enough?"

Dr. Arthur had the nerve to chuckle. "Well, that supports my belief from my last exam that your baby is almost here. The fetus should be large enough by now to be moving quite a bit. That's a wonderful sign. It sounds like you have a strong, healthy child on the way."

Oh my God. There's still so much more we need to do to get ready. "So, you're saying it could be any minute?"

The doctor's laughter was heartier. Vic wanted to punch him.

"It's possible, but I doubt it. If the egg is only moving now for the first time, what it means is that your baby is building up it's strength to push their way out of the shell. He or she will need some more time to do that, but you're definitely getting closer. I'd estimate about a week or so from this point."

Vic let out a relieved sigh. That still gave them more time and he was also relieved that the doctor seemed to have a clearer picture of the situation than he'd had when he'd last checked the egg.

"Okay, great. That's good to know, thank you." He shifted on his feet. "Sorry I got so snippy there. I'm not used to, you know, this parent thing."

"Oh, don't worry about it. At least you didn't try to peck my eyes out!"

Vic snorted. "True. But we appreciate everything you're doing for us."

They said their goodbyes and Vic rushed back to the bedroom to pass on the news to Kellan.

Kellan's eyes rounded as Vic shared what Dr. Arthur had told him. "Oh no. I still need so many baby things!"

His forehead creased with worry and Vic rubbed his chin through his beard, contemplating what they could do. "Well, if it's all right with you, sweetheart, I could take over nesting duties again tomorrow and you could get some more shopping time in. How does that sound?"

Judging from Kellan's slumped shoulders, he didn't think Kellan was that thrilled with his suggestion.

"I think it's very nice of you, Vic. But since I don't drive, and the bus only goes to the one department store..."

"Right." Vic nodded. Not only would Kellan have limited shopping options, but how would he carry a bunch of items by himself? "What if we got someone else to stay with the egg while you and I...?" Vic swallowed hard at the glare directed at him from Kellan. "Not for very long, just so we could..." He coughed into his fist. "Never mind." Vic shoved his hands in his jean pockets. "There're always online stores."

Kellan appeared crestfallen. "I never thought too hard about this. I guess I should've realized all along that we'd have to do most of our shopping online because of the egg." Kellan fidgeted on the bed. "I wish the Christmas Market was still happening. There were so many cute, handmade items there. Special things we could've gotten for the baby."

Dora spoke up. "Look, I know I'm a poor substitute, but I have an idea. Why don't *I* take Kellan shopping? We could drive to the big mall about an hour from here, then on the way back, we can visit my cousin's shop a couple towns over. She and her wife have the coolest boutique with lots of crocheted, quilted and knitted items. All handmade." She gazed up at the ceiling. "Of course, *someone* would have to give me the day off."

"Yeah, *someone* would." Vic chuckled as he turned to Kellan. "Well, what do you think?"

Kellan broke into a smile. "Can we, Vic? That would be amazing. I could even send you pics of things so you can help pick them out, just as if you were there!"

"Of course, you can. But I'm sure whatever you choose will be fine." Vic smiled back.

"But I want you to be a part of everything for the baby too."

Vic wasn't sure what the big deal was, but he could tell how important it was to Kellan and that was what mattered. "Then I'll be anxiously waiting to see the pics."

Kellan's smile grew bigger and he and Dora immediately fell into making plans for their big excursion the next day.

Skip elbowed him and Vic realized he'd almost forgotten his cook was there in the room.

"Now that *that's* taken care of, any chance I can get some coffee?"

Vic snorted as he shook his head. "Yes, Skip. Help yourself."

As Skip ambled his way to the kitchen, Vic tried to imagine what their lives would be like once the baby arrived. He spied the toy wolf they'd bought at the Christmas market, the one he'd set next to the egg after Kellan had first laid it. Would their child have his coat the way Kellan wanted? Or would the baby be all swan?

A thread of excitement coursed through him again. He couldn't wait to find out.

CHAPTER FOUR

*K*ellan was very proud of himself. He'd only called Vic twice to check on the egg and only done one video call so Vic could show him the egg was okay. He didn't think he'd done too badly, considering he and Dora had been gone for almost six hours. Of course, that didn't count the endless pictures of baby items he'd sent so Vic could help him decide on what to purchase. It was funny how much they were the same. Every single thing he said he liked, Vic said he liked it too.

The piles of bags containing the new things for the baby, plus a special present for Vic, were carefully stashed in the trunk of Dora's sporty compact car. Fortunately, they'd been able to fit the unassembled cradle in the back seat. The countryside flew by as they traveled on one of the back roads headed to Vale Valley, and Kellan couldn't stop fidgeting in his seat. The pull of his nest had begun to nag at him right as they had finished their shopping.

"Are you sure you're okay, Kel? We could head straight back to Vale and go to my cousin's place another time."

"No, that's okay. I really want to go. It sounds as if they have the kinds of things I was looking for. You know, handmade and special."

Dora patted his arm. "As long as you're fine with still going. But tell me if you decide you want to leave. They won't mind and neither will I. Promise?"

"I promise."

He hoped he could last long enough to at least pick up a crocheted blanket or maybe an embroidered onesie. The past hour had become increasingly uncomfortable, as if there was a slight itch underneath his skin, one that was barely discernible, but all over his body at the same time.

"So," Dora began. "What's your favorite thing you got at the mall?"

Kellan bit his lip. He may or may not have overspent. "I love everything, but the fuzzy blue jacket is perfect." It was a deep jewel blue, puffy, soft and lined with fleece. If it had come in his size, he'd have bought one for himself. "But I don't think anything could be more amazing than the cradle."

Dora nodded, but kept her eyes trained on the road. It hadn't snowed that day and the roads were plowed with added gravel, but it was still icy in spots.

"Yeah, I'd have to agree. I've never seen anything quite like that. It reminds me of an antique Dutch one the way it's enclosed and with how intricate the woodwork is." She let out a low whistle. "It was priced like an antique too." She grinned.

Kellan chewed on his lip even harder. "It was the only one enclosed like that. Swan shifter babies like the feel of the nest after they're hatched. I didn't know what else to do." He put a hand to his forehead. "Maybe I should've waited."

Dora sighed. "I shouldn't have said anything. Kel, it's fine. You showed it to Vic, he loved it, told you to get it. What are you worried about? And you can't exactly wait anymore. Dr. Arthur said the baby will be here soon."

"But I didn't tell Vic how much it was, only that it was expensive."

"Kel, seriously. You need to stop already. Don't you think if Vic was worried how much it cost, he would've asked you the price? You said expensive, he said if you like it then get it. Not, 'how much is it'."

What Dora said made complete sense, yet he couldn't help but fret over the bags upon bags upon boxes he had stuffed everywhere in Dora's car.

"Dora? You've known Vic for a while. Do you think he's really happy about the baby?"

Her jaw dropped and she gasped. "I can't believe you said that! Do you have any idea how terribly alone he's been all these years? With no family anymore after he lost his pack?"

Kellan hung his head. "I know, but everything *has* happened awfully fast. And we didn't think we could ever have any children at all because of him being a wolf, so we didn't plan for it. That's all I mean. Maybe he feels rushed into everything." Kellan sighed. "I just love him so much and I don't want him to be unhappy."

"Kel, I think the asshat who had the nerve to call himself your brother has made you doubt everything too much. You're an omega. He's an Alpha. You're fated mates. What the hell else did you guys think was gonna happen when you fucked?"

"Dora!" Kellan's face flushed hot. "I can't believe you said that."

"Basic biology, hon." She snorted. "But for real, you're right about one thing. I *have* known Vic for a while, and that was one lonely wolf. He was always smiling and friendly, it wasn't that. But there was a look in his eyes, a dark cloud as if he was haunted by all the horrible memories of his past, as if he couldn't banish them no matter how successful he became or how many friends he made." A gentle smile tugged at the corner of her lips. "That all changed when he found you."

Kellan blinked several times as he took in her words. Vic had reassured him over and over of his love, but Kellan still couldn't let go of his fears, his insecurities borne of the bullshit Finn had always flung at him. He frowned to himself. He needed to knock it off and focus on giving Vic all his love and accepting it in return without question. Vic deserved that.

They drove in silence for a while until Dora signaled at a turn that didn't seem to go anywhere, except into desolate woodland like the scenery they'd been driving past.

"Is this where your cousin lives?"

"Yeah." Dora made a right down a narrow two-lane road. "It's off the beaten path for sure. Only a couple hundred residents, and they keep to themselves." She elbowed him. "Mainly shifters who prefer seclusion."

"Oh, I see." Kellan gazed out the window, but still couldn't see any signs that they were near anything. "Are they all bobcat shifters?"

"No, but there are quite a few. We have some foxes, a few squirrels, rabbits. You know, the local wildlife."

Kellan's eyes widened. "And they all get along? They don't try to kill each other?"

Dora shook her head. "Shifters are fiercely loyal to each other. There are so few of us and there's safety in numbers. If we kill each other off, we're only making ourselves weaker. To be honest, it's why I moved to Vale Valley. I've been trying to convince my family that the magic protecting the valley would keep them safer than if they stay out here and tough it out on their own." Dora shrugged. "But I can't force them to do what I want."

Kellan considered what she'd told him. "Gosh, I suppose I hadn't thought of that. The other thing Finn always drummed into me was not to trust anyone, not even other shifters—especially the predator ones. He said they would kill and eat us the first chance they got."

Kellan shuddered as he recalled the night Vic found him. It might have ended up being the best night of his life, but when he first saw Vic's wolf, he'd thought he was toast.

Dora let out a small growl. "Is it all right if I kick your brother's ass if I ever see him?"

Kellan laughed. He could only imagine what a sight that would be. Dora didn't put up with any nonsense. He'd seen her in action when she'd had to deal with unruly customers or a cranky Skip at the restaurant.

They reached the end of the road they were on and were left with the choice to turn right or left. There weren't any signs to indicate which way was which, but Dora undoubtedly knew where she was headed when she signaled to the left. After they were headed in the new direction, Kellan noticed the occasional dirt road breaking the endless wall of evergreens, along with bare-limbed maple and birch trees reaching up from the thick piles of snow, the paths leading the way into the woods to some unknown destination.

As he craned his neck to see what was ahead, a few structures huddled together in the distance drew closer.

"Is that the town coming up?"

She chuckled. "Such as it is, yeah. Post office, small market, gas station and my cousin's place."

"And all she sells is baby stuff?"

"Big people need blankets and sweaters too." Dora cleared her throat. "But you can also use the copy machine, buy office supplies and get keys made."

Kellan arched his eyebrows. "I guess that's what you've gotta do in such a small town."

"Yeah, her wife handles that part of the business. And actually, Lena sells a lot of her creations online. Convenient to have the post office right next door."

Kellan nodded. "I'll say."

They reached the strip of buildings that housed the businesses in the town Dora informed him was named Bobcat Stump, the gas station boasting one pump at the far end. Diagonal parking spaces were angled to the right, the painted stripes allowing for a few cars to have a spot in front of each address, the wood slat buildings a brick red with white window and door trim. Dora pulled her car into one of the spaces by the shop with a sign in the window declaring it to be Lena Sue's Craft & Office.

"Here we are! I told her we were on our way before we left the mall so she'd get the place heated up." Dora pushed the car door open. "They don't come in town that much in the winter, only if she has orders to ship out."

Kellan stepped out of the vehicle, careful of the slippery areas. "I hope I'm not being too much trouble."

He followed Dora up the salted walkway to the front of the store, the shop's door solid wood until right above the brass latch where the window glass took over the remainder of the rustic barrier.

"No, not at all. It's quiet and can get lonely up here. This has been a great excuse for me to come and visit." She glanced over her shoulder. "I get so caught up in my own life in Vale Valley sometimes—you know, working non-stop, my new boyfriend. You're doing me a favor, Kel." She sighed as she reached for the latch. "I should come by more often."

As they entered the quaint building with hardwood floors, the warmth of the room hit Kellan in the face, a welcome contrast to the bitter cold of the outside. It might not have been a long walk from the comfort of the car, but it had been enough to give him a chill. He tugged off his knit cap then stuffed it into his pocket. The floor creaked and before he had the chance to comment on how cool and colorful all the items were, a woman's voice called from somewhere in the back behind a row of glass showcases.

"Dora? Is that you and your friend?"

An attractive woman with shoulder-length hair the color of auburn, big round eyes and very pale, freckled skin, pushed through a curtain hanging in the doorway leading to what had to be the stockroom.

Dora rushed forward with her arms outstretched until she and who Kellan presumed was her cousin met on the other side of the display cases. They grabbed each other in a hug, their excited greetings tumbling out as they jabbered on with 'it's so great to see you', 'how long has it been?', 'how's everyone doing?' and more that Kellan couldn't discern.

Wow. A real family.

He and Vic would have that. Their babies would grow up and make families of their own with cousins and aunts and uncles and everything.

And we'll be grandparents.

Everyone would love one another, and they would care whether one of them was hurting or whether they needed help. Kellan grinned as he let his mind wander, imagining the scenarios of picnics, parties and holidays that could be shared with their beautiful clan.

"Kel? I said this is Lena, my cousin."

Kellan blinked a few times as he brought himself back to the present.

"Oh! I'm sorry." He held out a hand to her. "Hi, Lena. Thank you for coming to your shop today so I could buy a few things." He gazed around the room. "Or maybe a lot of things."

Lena chuckled, giving Kellan's had a few shakes before letting go. "Not a problem at all. It's good to warm up the place once in a while. You take your time and look around. I'll make us all some cocoa and me and Dora can get caught up while you shop."

"Thanks." Kellan waited until Lena had headed to the back before turning to Dora. "She's really nice. Is your whole family like that?"

"Oh yeah." She gave a light laugh. "Especially when they're not getting on my nerves."

Kellan arched his eyebrows. "I don't understand. Some of them aren't nice people?"

"Don't get me wrong, I love them all. It's not that. But we all have our own personalities and quirks. Just because we're related and would do anything for each other, doesn't mean they don't annoy me now and then. Especially my little brother, Darren. What a pain in the ass he can be!"

Kellan's mouth formed an 'O'. "But you love him anyway?"

Dora grinned as she snorted out laughter. "Of course. I just tease him relentlessly until he shuts up."

"Gosh." *This whole family thing is a lot more complicated than I realized.*

"Hon? Families aren't perfect. They bicker and complain, sometimes cry or don't speak for a while, but most of the time, they're the ones who will be there for you when others aren't. What matters is that they back you up and, most importantly, are the ones whose love you can always count on."

Kellan nodded. "I see. I guess I've only experienced family when it's been one extreme or the other—not the middle parts."

She gave him a pat on his arm. "That's okay. You'll figure it out. Just remember that the love you share is what's most important."

Lena emerged from behind the curtain again with a tray of mugs then set them on one of the cases. After taking a few sips of the chocolate, Kellan left Dora and Lena to their conversation and made his way to the boutique section of the shop. Every item was beautifully handcrafted, and he made a promise to himself that he would come back another time to buy an afghan for the couch and a quilt for their bed. He also spotted a beautiful scarlet red knit sweater that would look stunning on Vic.

Maybe for Valentine's Day?

But for now, he needed to focus on why they'd come to Bobcat Stump. It was all about their baby and nothing else.

After selecting a knitted blanket in an alternating pattern of blues and greens, two knitted caps, an indigo sweater and several pairs of booties, Kellan not only felt he'd annihilated his spending limit, but was no longer able to resist the pull of his nest. He needed to get home.

Dora gathered up the bag with the blanket and sweater and Kellan grabbed the one with the caps and booties.

"Tell Darren I said he's a dork and I promise to come up for the annual spring equinox get-together."

Lena bellowed out laughter. "You'd better, or we'll come and kidnap you." She regarded Kellan. "Congratulations on your little hatchling-to-be and I hope we see you again soon."

"Thanks. And you will. I saw other things I want to get next time."

Lena winked at him. "I saw you eyeing that sweater. Is it for your mate?"

Kellan flushed. "Yeah. He'd be even more handsome in it than he already is."

She chuckled. "I'll put it aside for you and you come back whenever you're ready."

"Really?"

She grinned. "Really."

"Thank you so much! If Dora comes to visit again in the next week or two, I can send the money with her."

Lena smirked at Dora. "Hear that? Now you don't have an excuse to stay away so long."

Dora protested to Lena that she hadn't been making excuses, that she'd been very busy and hadn't realized how long it had been since her last visit. She continued to protest her innocence as she followed Kellan to the door. Right as he opened it, a cry for help echoed across the parking lot in the direction of the gas station.

It can't be.

Kellan marched toward the commotion without thinking, some sort of hidden spark of rage within him he hadn't known existed igniting in his veins, driving him forward, driving him to make things right the way he should have years before.

"Hey! Finn! What do you think you're doing, you big bully?"

His brother whipped around, releasing the collar of the shirt the young man who was crying for help was wearing. The man crumpled to the ground and crawled away, whimpering.

"The fuck?" Finn squinted at him. "You're not dead?"

Kellan hissed, the fury in him rising. He'd always known deep down Finn had meant for him to die, but to hear him say it to his face as if it was no big deal made Kellan want to pluck Finn's feathers and leave him at the mercy of Dora's bobcat relatives.

No. This is my fight.

"Very *much* alive, despite your best efforts. I guess you're not as brilliant as you've always told yourself you are."

Finn spit on the ground. "And you're just as stupid as ever. I'm going to make sure I personally finish the job this time."

Dora rushed up behind him, breathless. "Kellan, don't. I can shift, so can Lena and Sue. We'll take him on so you don't have to."

Right then, two members of his ex-herd ran out of the market, a satchel in their hands. "Come on, Finn. We got everything in the register plus some guns, let's get the fuck outta here!"

The hissing built inside Kellan, all the anger and hurt of

many, many years ready to explode out of him. He shoved his bag at Dora.

"Hold my booties."

Kellan tore off his jacket and clothes, toeing off his boots as Finn snarled at him and did the same. He shifted and the battle cry of '*swan fight!*' could be heard from behind him. He threw open his wings to their full expanse, rising on his webbed feet and stretching his long neck in a display of aggression. Finn snarled then shifted, following suit. They circled each other, squawking and hissing and Kellan flapped his wings furiously, his swan taking over and leading the charge as he pounced on Finn.

A flurry of feathers erupted as they thrashed and tangled, the solid bone of a wing joint connecting with Kellan's eye and sending him backward. He fell with a *thump* on his back with Finn jumping on him, beating him with his wings in an effort to land another blow while Kellan clawed at him with the nails of his feet. They rolled in a jumble of scratching, pecking and more flapping.

Get him! Evil! Bad swan, bad swan!

Kellan got his feet back under him then used the power of his wings to catch the air and propel himself back. He needed some space to get a running start so he could finish things off. As Finn righted himself, Kellan struck, charging at him with every ounce of righteous anger that he possessed. He lashed out at Finn, slamming both wing joints against Finn's head, watching in satisfaction as Finn fell to the ground.

A trickle of blood trailed from Finn's head, between his eyes and landed on his beak. He attempted to scramble to his feet again, but one of his wings must have been broken, because he listed to one side before crumpling into a battered heap.

"You're dead, worm food!"

Kellan's swan readied himself to battle Ardus, one of Finn's minions and no less deserving of Kellan's wrath. He spread his wings to their full expanse, but the growls and snarls of bobcats at his back stayed his advance. Two bobcats appeared on either side of him, while three more crept up behind Ardus, Taryn and the injured Finn. Kellan recognized Dora and Lena as two of his supporters.

Kellan shifted back to his human form. "I don't think you're welcome here anymore." He spit out some blood from a cut in his mouth. "My friends won't hesitate to rip you to pieces and it seems you're outnumbered."

Ardus and Taryn helped a disoriented Finn to his feet. Finn sputtered and coughed.

"My omega! Where the fuck is he?"

His omega? Oh hell no. "Get out of here, *now*."

Ardus hoisted the satchel he'd stolen over his shoulder as they made their way to the very pick-up truck Finn had shoved him out of on a snowy night in November.

"And leave that, you filthy thief."

Ardus sneered over his shoulder. "Fuck you."

Dora howled then bounded toward him. Ardus yelped, dropped the bag then raced for the truck, not even waiting to help Taryn with Finn. The bobcats kept up their chorus of snarls and yowls until his brother and rotten ex-herd members were well on their way. It wasn't until everyone had shifted back and his adrenaline rush had begun to wane that he wondered whether they should've turned them in to the authorities.

"Oh my gods, Kellan. Your eye. Vic is going to have a complete fit." Dora stared at him with concern.

He raised his hand to check it, but a sharp pain radiated from his elbow. "Ow, damn."

Dora put a hand on his back. "Come on, hon. Let's gather up our clothes and get you back inside the store so we can look you over. Lena's in there with Sean, the guy you saved from whom I'm guessing was your brother and the herd you told me about."

Kellan picked up his clothes while Dora did the same with hers but hurried into his boots first thing to avoid the icy burn of the ground against the soles of his feet. Once they were inside the store and reasonably back to rights, Kellan voiced his worry over letting Finn go.

Lena shook her head after he'd made his case. "We'll put our own people on it, get the word out through the shifter network. This isn't like that special place you and Dora live in. We have to be more careful out here. Dora got the plates of the truck, so we'll be keeping an eye out. Human law going after shifter criminals never works out well. All he has to do is turn into a swan and there you are. Tough to accuse a large waterfowl of robbing your convenience store."

Kellan let out a frustrated sigh. "He shouldn't keep getting away with it all the time." He frowned as he glanced around the shop. "Didn't you say the guy who was crying for help is in here?"

Lena jerked her head toward the curtain. "He's in the back room with Sue. She had just arrived right as everything went tits up. He'd like to thank you and..." Lena glanced at Dora who shrugged her shoulders. "We were thinking. Since you're a swan, and apparently, *he's* a swan, maybe he'd like to go back to Vale Valley with you?"

"I don't understand. Wouldn't he rather go home? You know, wherever that is?"

Dora chewed on her thumbnail. "You should go talk to him. It doesn't sound like he has one."

Oh no. What did Finn do this time?

"Okay, I guess I could do that." He worried his lip. "What should I say?"

Dora shrugged. "I dunno. Go with your swan senses."

Kellan narrowed his eyes at her. If he'd had any swan sense, he would've gotten away from Finn a lot sooner than he had.

"You're a big help." His shoulders slumped. "Wish me luck, I guess."

Dora gave him an encouraging smile. "You'll do great. In the meantime, we'll make more cocoa."

Kellan rolled his eyes. *Cocoa.* He made his way behind the counter and past the curtain where he spotted the young man Finn had been manhandling. *Sean.* He sat on a floral couch with his denim-clad legs tucked beneath him, wearing a torn navy-blue sweater that was at least two sizes too big. He didn't have a jacket. His honey blond hair was longer in the front and hung in his eyes. Sean appeared to be about his age and was at least as small as he was as well.

He glanced up as Kellan approached with large, round caramel colored eyes framed by dark lashes. His skin was as porcelain as Kellan's and he had a stray thought that they seemed as if they could be related based on looks alone.

"Hi, Sean. I'm Kellan. Is it okay if I sit down next to you? I'm a little sore after all that."

Sean hiccupped on a sob. "Please, sit. I'm so sorry you got hurt because of me. I don't want anyone else to *ever* get hurt again because of me."

Kellan perched on the edge of the cushion. "Well, I don't think that'll happen, so you shouldn't worry."

"But what if he comes back? What if he returns with the rest of the herd and tries to take me and hurts other people?"

Kellan squirmed on the couch. He wasn't usually the one doing the reassuring. "I don't know if you saw or not, but I whooped his ass and he seemed to be in a pretty big hurry when he left."

Sean straightened a bit. A smile tugged at the corner of his mouth. "That really happened?"

Kellan snorted. "Yeah, I can barely believe it myself. But it's for real. And anyway, he's nothing but a big bully. He's not as tough as he thinks he is."

Sean hung his head, and after a moment of silence, Kellan realized he was crying.

"Oh no. Did I say something wrong?" Kellan twisted his hands in his lap. "I'm sorry. I'm not very good at making people feel better, I guess."

Sean shook his head and wiped the back of his hand under his nose. "Finn killed my best friend and forced me to go with him and the herd."

Killed? Sure, Finn and the gang had robbed their way across the Eastern seaboard and all the way to the Canadian border, but he'd never known them to be murderers.

"That's awful, Sean. I know Finn's a horrible, horrible being, but why would he kill your friend?"

Sean lifted his gaze. "Because he wanted me to be his... you know. I'm an omega, but my best friend was an Alpha and when he wouldn't take Finn up on his offer that we join them, he stabbed Gary, right in front of me."

Sean dropped his head in his hands and sobbed openly. Kellan swallowed hard, shocked to discover that his brother was even more despicable than he'd thought. *Now we* have *to get the shifter network after him.* Being a thief was one thing, but a killer? No, Finn had to be brought down before he murdered another innocent person.

Kellan regarded the hurt swan sitting next to him and remembered how scared and lonely he'd been when Vic had found him. *And I hadn't even been through something as terrible as Sean.*

He dared to place a hand on Sean's arm. "Everything's going to be all right, Sean, I promise. We're taking you to Vale Valley. You'll be safe there."

CHAPTER FIVE

*V*ic dozed on the bed, his body curled around the base of the nest with one hand resting against the egg. His eyes fluttered open, and he frowned at the realization that darkness had fallen.

That's odd.

He rolled onto his back and reached for his cell that he'd laid on the nightstand. When he woke it up, he saw that it was almost six, which meant Kellan was an hour past when he'd said he'd be home, and no messages had come in either. His mate had been gone close to seven hours, which was fine, except Kellan had been in constant contact with him all day, so the lack of communication left him concerned.

Vic sat up and arranged the blankets around and over the top of the egg so he could stoke the fire in the living room. He'd taken an hour break in the middle of the day to grab some lunch and use the bathroom, but he'd never left the cabin. The one time he and Kellan had left the egg alone had been on New Year's Eve for a staff party at the restaurant, but it hadn't lasted more than an hour. When he'd been unable to find Kellan amongst the partiers, he'd discovered him back at their cabin with the egg. Kellan had made it clear that from then on, one of them had to stay with the nest at all times.

Where the hell is he?

Vic added a couple more pieces of wood to the fire then poked at them to stir up the embers. He glanced up from his task as the glow of headlights shone through the small window to the right of the door. After placing the fire poker back in the stand, he rushed to grab his jacket and yank on his boots in the entryway. From the shopping report Kellan had been sharing with him all day, he imagined there would be quite a number of purchases he'd need to haul in from Dora's car.

With a happy smile, he tugged open the door then came to an abrupt halt.

The fuck?

In front of Dora's car stood a small man who was no bigger than Kellan and was also wearing Kellan's winter coat. Kellan placed an arm around his shoulder and encouraged him forward. When they stepped under the glow of the porchlight, Vic gasped. A deep, low growl rumbled from his chest at the sight of bruises on the young man's face then turned to a full snarl when his gaze landed on Kellan.

The young man whimpered, cowering and hiding his face against Kellan's shoulder. Kellan wrapped a protective arm over the man, clutching him to his body.

"Vic, you're scaring him!"

He didn't care. All he wanted to know was why he was there and why the *hell* Kellan had a swollen eye and scratches on both cheeks. Vic looked past them to Dora who remained a few steps back and near her car. She averted her gaze. Vic drew his eyebrows together as he noted that both she and her car appeared unscathed.

They weren't in an accident, apparently.

Dora cleared her throat. "I think I'll head over to the inn and hang out for a bit so you all can have a chat. You know, alone." She tucked her hair behind her ears and laughed uneasily. "Helluva day."

Vic growled again. "So it would seem."

He returned his attention to Kellan and his apparent friend. The ache to hold Kellan and make sure he was okay was agonizing, but he supposed he should get caught up on the day's events first. Whoever the man was that Kellan had brought home appeared to be in trouble. Leave it to his kind-hearted mate to try and help.

Vic regarded Dora. "Yeah, I'd appreciate a moment or two to get clued in. I'll text you when we're done so I can get Kellan's things unloaded from your car."

She gave him a thumbs up then hurried toward the inn. Vic waved Kellan and his friend inside in what he hoped wouldn't come across as too threatening to the injured stranger. He could smell the fear from them both, but he assumed Kellan's was related to whether Vic would be mad at him.

"Come on, sweetheart. Let's get you and your friend out of the cold."

Kellan's shoulders relaxed, his expression brightening, and Vic realized he'd called it right. *I don't want him ever to be afraid of coming to me.*

"Thanks, Vic." Kellan gazed up at him with grateful eyes.

Vic stood to the side of the threshold to allow them to pass through without him looming over the still frightened stranger. While Kellan got his friend settled on the couch, Vic added some more wood to the fire. He needed to keep the egg warm and he worried he'd get distracted by whatever surprise revelations Kellan had in store for him.

As soon as he turned around Kellan was there, his arms open and bottom lip trembling. Vic smiled and gathered him in a firm embrace. He might still be upset over seeing Kellan hurt, but was filled with joy at having him back home. Vic kissed the top of his head then held him back by his shoulders so he could look him over.

He pressed his lips together, swallowing down another growl at the sight of Kellan's swollen eye and the scratches across his skin. Fortunately, none of them seemed very deep, but they should still be cleaned. Vic tugged at the bottom of Kellan's pullover sweater, anxious to inspect him for any other injuries.

"Any sprains or cuts I can't see?"

"I bumped my right wing joint—I mean elbow—pretty hard. It might need an ice pack and a wrap. And that jerk cut my leg pretty bad, but Lena cleaned and wrapped it for me. She said I don't need any stitches."

Vic sucked in a sharp breath as he assisted Kellan with the removal of the sweater as gently as he could. He didn't want to let out a series of curses and yells, but he was having to use all his willpower not to. Finally, the forest green garment was removed, and Vic could immediately see how swollen his elbow was. He took a few calming breaths as he glanced over at the young man on the couch who was now curled up in a fetal position, Kellan's jacket collar wrapped around his jaw so it covered most of his face.

He leaned down to whisper in Kellan's ear, "Is he all right? I mean, *physically*? Maybe we should take him to Vale General."

Kellan shook his head. "No, he's been getting beaten by Finn and the rest of the herd a lot, but they're only bruises and stuff. Nothing broken."

Vic gasped, straightening. "*What*? What do you mean *Finn*?" Vic snarled and snapped. "Where is he? I'll kill him!"

He launched himself toward the door, only vaguely taking in the sounds of the crying man on the couch and Kellan's protests to wait. He flung the door wide, a loud snap resounding as wood cracked under the force of his anger. He shifted in an instant, clawing at the clothes he hadn't had time to remove, his fury driving him on as he broke free of the garments. He leaped across the parking lot in a rage, his only thought being one of reaching Dora so she could guide him to the swan he was about to rip to shreds.

"Vic, *please*! Please don't leave me here alone!"

His paws skidded across the ice and he rammed into a pile of snow that had been pushed against the side of the restaurant from when they'd repeatedly plowed. He hit hard against the solid mass, but the recent powder cushioned some of the blow. His wolf warned him that he'd be feeling it in his shoulder by morning.

He shook his body to get the excess snow out of his fur then scrambled to his four paws. His wolf still tasted blood, still hungered for revenge, but the insistent cries of his omega kept him from continuing on his murderous mission. Vic threw back his head, letting out one mournful howl before trotting back to his mate.

Once he'd padded inside, he shifted back. He glanced around in dismay at the mess he'd made, the shredded clothes everywhere mixed in with splinters of wood. *Dammit.* Fortunately, his explosion of anger had drained some of his wolf's wrath and he figured he'd now be rational enough to listen to poor Kellan who was staring at him with rounded eyes his lips parted in shock.

His first action needed to include reassuring his mate. "Sweetheart, I'm sorry. Please forgive me for that outburst. I just can't bear the thought that Finn managed to get to you, and I wasn't there to keep you safe."

"Oh, Vic. Don't be sorry." Kellan ran to him, throwing his arms around Vic's naked waist. He peered up at him and, to Vic's surprise, he was smiling. "Don't worry. I kicked the crap out of him."

Vic sputtered laughter. "You did?"

He couldn't stand it any longer and despite the cold draft that was literally freezing his ass off, he claimed Kellan's mouth in a deep kiss, tasted the heat and sweetness of the man he would die for. Vic ended the exchange with one final press to Kellan's lips then straightened.

"I guess I should quit acting like a rabid dog and hear what happened before we go any further." He peered over his shoulder. "Although, I need to get this door shut somehow against the cold and your elbow attended too first."

Kellan jerked from his arms. "The egg!"

Without another word, Kellan was racing to the nest and, after a quick glance at their unexpected guest who'd gone back to cowering on the couch, he set about the task of wrestling the heavy door back into the frame, relieved that he'd only torn one hinge free. Once he latched it with the bolt, that and the remaining hinge kept it in place. He'd be stuck unloading Dora's car from the side entrance, but it was his own damn fault for flipping out.

For the next half hour, Vic focused on putting things to rights and getting them back on track. He cleaned up the mess he'd made in the entryway, guaranteed the fire was roaring and was attending to Kellan's elbow by bringing him an ice pack and holding it to his injury so he was free to be close to the egg. Kellan was sitting up with the egg between his legs and his body wrapped around it. Vic had placed a cushioning of blankets under Kellan's right arm so the cold radiating from the pack wouldn't be transferred to the shell.

Vic used his free hand to stroke Kellan's back. "How are you feeling?"

Kellan's cheek rested on top of the egg. "My elbow's throbbing and my eye hurts. But I'm okay. I'm sure the painkiller you gave me will help."

Vic nodded, determined to remain calm even as his wolf's anger fought to rise to the surface. "Right before I came in here with the ice, I noticed our guest seems to have fallen asleep on the couch. Are you sure he shouldn't be checked out by a doctor?"

"I'm sure. Lena and Dora looked him over before we left Bobcat Stump."

Vic arched his eyebrows. He really needed to be brought up to speed. The pack had been on Kellan's elbow for at least fifteen minutes, so he removed the ice and set it on the nightstand. Once he'd retrieved the wrap, he encouraged Kellan to lift his arm enough so he could apply the self-sticking cloth. It also afforded him a moment to gather his thoughts. He had at least a thousand questions.

"All right, then before we go any further, I need to hear the whole story. Since we spoke right as you were leaving the mall, I assume this saga began in the afore-mentioned Bobcat Stump?"

Kellan chewed on the side of his lip, gazing at Vic as if he wasn't sure whether Vic might get mad again. "Yeah. That's the place I told you Dora was taking me to get some special, hand-crafted baby items. Lena is her cousin who makes them."

Vic nodded. "And how does..." Vic drew his eyebrows together. "What's the name of the guy on our couch?"

"That's Sean. Sean Swanson."

Vic lifted an eyebrow. "*Swan*son?"

"Yeah, why? Do you know any Swansons?"

Vic sighed, rubbing his forehead. "Uh, no. Never mind. So anyway, can you tell me everything that happened? I'm not mad at you and I won't be no matter what you say. A lot of my behavior is from the anger at myself for not being there when you needed me. I'm supposed to be protecting my family, not leaving them to be attacked."

Kellan lifted his head and rubbed his cheek against Vic's arm.

"But you *did* protect your family. You were here watching over our egg and keeping it safe."

Vic swallowed past a lump in his throat. "You're right, sweetheart. I suppose I did." He rubbed slow circles on Kellan's back. "Then tell me the whole story of what went on at Bobcat Stump and how my brave swan saved the day."

~

*K*ellan checked once more to make sure the blankets were securely wrapped around the egg. He doubted it would be much of an issue, though. Vic had gotten the cabin's temperature high enough that all of them—even Sean —were wearing nothing but T-shirts and boxers. Of course, that had only been after Vic had dragged everything in from the car and they'd said their goodbyes to Dora.

I think he took things pretty well.

His main concern had been that Vic would be angry but his mate had reassured him that he wasn't upset with him in the slightest.

Kellan ambled into the living room to check on Sean. The poor guy had been through so much already, and he was sure Vic's rather dramatic performance had only served to scare him half to death. Sure enough, Sean was pressed against the arm of the couch that was the farthest from where Vic was puttering in the kitchen. After Kellan had finished his sordid tale, Vic had given him a toe-curling kiss then excused himself so he could make them all some hot cider and put together a snack. Sean appeared as skinny as he'd been when Vic had first rescued him.

Kellan approached Sean gingerly. "Hey. Is it okay if I sit down?"

Sean gazed up at him in confusion, almost as if he'd forgotten who he was. He seemed to regain his senses. "Yeah, of course. This is your home and I'm the intruder."

Oh dear. Kellan took a seat. "Don't say that, Sean. That's not how I feel at all."

Sean glanced past him at Vic. Kellan peered over his shoulder, tracking Sean's gaze and noting that Vic was busily preparing things and oblivious to anything they were doing. Kellan kept his voice low.

"You don't have to be afraid of my mate. Vic is an amazing guy. He loves me and our egg very much and went all Alpha nutso because someone hurt us. But he's not upset at *you*, I promise."

Sean stared at Kellan open-mouthed. "You have an egg of your very own?"

Kellan smiled, relieved that Sean seemed ready to communicate. "Uh-huh. Vic's my fated mate and we have a hatchling on the way." Kellan's smile deepened as his cheeks flushed. "We're engaged too."

Sean's gaze darted to Vic again before landing back on Kellan. "I don't want you to think I'm being rude, but was it Vic who fertilized the egg?"

Kellan's knee-jerk reaction was to be insulted, but he had to admit he'd wondered the same thing at first. "I know, we were surprised too. I think it's because we're fated that we'll soon have a baby."

"That's incredible. You're so lucky." He stared at Kellan in awe. "Do you know if he or she will be a swan or a wolf? Or both?"

Kellan shrugged. "No idea. But we have an avian fertility specialist helping us out. He and his wife are eagle shifters." He furrowed his brow. "Oh, and his nephew, Avi, is Vale Valley's new fire chief."

On the drive back from Bobcat Stump, Kellan and Dora has

already filled Sean in on Vale Valley and how it would be the safest place for him to be while he recovered from his ordeal with Finn and the herd. Kellan hadn't had the chance to give Vic all the grisly details of Sean's captivity, but he'd let him know that Sean desperately needed their help.

Before they had a chance to continue their conversation, Vic entered the room with a tray of three mugs, each one containing a cinnamon stick stirrer in addition to the cider and a plate of oatmeal raisin cookies. He set everything down on the coffee table before taking a seat in the chair across from the couch.

"Here you go. Help yourself."

Vic gave them a stiff smile, and Kellan could tell how uncomfortable he was. He was sure his reaction stemmed from how sorry he was that his behavior had caused Sean to be even more afraid than he already was.

Kellan handed one of the mugs to Sean then took a sip from his own to get things going. He arched his eyebrows at Vic who finally got the message to pick up his drink too. Kellan didn't want Sean to feel self-conscious.

Once they'd taken a few minutes to have some cider and cookies, Vic cleared his throat. "I know this isn't very much to eat. Kellan and I usually get our meals from the restaurant. I'm guessing he explained all that to you already? That the inn and restaurant is our place?"

Kellan sat a bit straighter, trying not to show his surprise that Vic had described the business as belonging to them both. He'd never thought of the inn as his and didn't know that was how Vic viewed their situation. He filed that tidbit away to discuss with his mate later.

Sean shook his head. "He said he'd bring me somewhere safe and that his mate—that you—had somewhere I could stay. But you don't have to. I don't want to be any trouble."

Vic scratched his chin through his beard. "No trouble. This is mine and Kellan's place and we have plenty of room. You're welcome to stay here in the cabin if you don't want to be alone, or we can set you up at the inn in your own space." Vic grinned. "I believe Kellan's old room is still empty."

Kellan regarded Sean. "And it has a nice view of the lake. But you can stay here with us if you'd rather."

Vic nodded. "Either way, I can order some food from the restaurant. We haven't had any dinner yet."

A tear trailed down Sean's face. "You're both so nice. Thank you very much." He regarded Kellan. "And I owe you my life, Kellan. I don't know how I'll ever repay you."

Kellan gave his new friend a hug. "You can get better and be happy. Everyone deserves that."

CHAPTER SIX

*T*he egg jerked again, and Kellan held his breath as he stared at it. *Valentine's Day is tomorrow. It's been almost two months since I laid the egg. Why hasn't our baby hatched yet?*

For the past week, the egg had moved al the time, but no cracks—not even the tiniest hairline of one. When Dr. Arthur had done his last exam, he'd said the egg hadn't grown anymore since the end of January, and that while the heartbeat of the baby was strong, he couldn't understand why the beginning stages of hatching hadn't begun yet. He'd mused that the wolf part of the baby might not understand how to break out of the shell to be born. However, there wasn't a way to know for sure.

Dr. Arthur had made one thing clear, however. Despite the dangers of transporting the egg to the hospital, he believed they'd have no other choice if the baby hadn't arrived by the day after Valentine's Day. At least at Vale General, they could do an ultrasound and if the baby appeared fully formed, they could crack the egg open in a controlled medical environment.

Kellan petted the shell, talking to their baby and pleading

with him or her to come out soon, that their daddies wanted to see and hold them so much. Having the egg hatch outside the nest and in someplace other than where it had been laid went against Kellan's swan sensibilities. He and his rotten brother had been born where they'd been laid in their nests, in one of the many homes they'd resided in during their nomadic upbringing. He knew from the other swans in the herd that they'd all been born in their nests too.

Where's Vic? Why is he taking so long?

He didn't want to be irritated with his mate, but he'd been on edge all week worrying about the egg. He'd even snapped at Vic one time, accusing him of not caring about their hatchling-to-be because he was so calm about everything. Boy, had he been ashamed when Vic had explained that he'd been trying to keep Kellan from worrying. It turned out Vic was as nervous about everything as Kellan was.

Kellan trailed a finger along the shell, from the tip of the blunted top down to the approximately one foot in diameter base. The egg seemed to jiggle in response to his touch. Kellan smiled. *The baby is fine. He or she is just a stubborn wolf like their father.* Kellan jerked upright, squinting his eyes. *Is that...?*

He gasped then turned up the brightness of the nightstand lamp. He stared at a tiny line at the very top of the egg, so thin that he tried to brush it away, assuming that it must be one of Vic's brown hairs.

But it couldn't be brushed away. It was a crack.

Kellan leaped from the bed and began jumping around the room. *What do I do? What do I do?* His heart raced and he grabbed his cell phone, the one Vic had bought him right after he'd laid the egg. *Vic. I have to call Vic.* But Vic would ask why he hadn't called Dr. Arthur first. *Right. Dr. Arthur.*

Kellan found the doctor's number in his contacts and tapped the button to call him. The number rang then it rang some more.

And still more. Dr. Arthur's voicemail answered, and Kellan wanted to hurl his phone against the wall. Instead, he left a message that was so garbled and frantic, Kellan doubted anyone would be able to understand one word. *That's all right. He'll see who called and figure it out.*

He rushed to the side of the bed again and got as close to the crack as he could without pressing his nose to the shell. *Is it bigger? Was it there earlier and I didn't notice?*

Frustration bubbled over and he did the only thing he could think of. He called everyone he knew, starting with 911 then Vic.

~

*V*ic sat in his truck outside of the Creatures of Comfort, tapping his fingers on the steering wheel. He'd already bought some new bath products and candles for Kellan that Flora had suggested he might enjoy. The romantic day he'd hoped to have with Kellan for their first Valentine's Day celebration didn't seem as though it would pan out. Somehow, he'd assumed the baby would have already arrived. His idea had been to have Dora stay with their newborn while they went to a fancy restaurant with live music and dancing, after which Vic would present Kellan with the custom-made platinum ring for their wedding.

I could give him the ring anyway, at home.

The egg was so overdue to hatch that neither one of them had left it alone for a single moment. No more wrapping their unborn baby in a blanket then sharing a bath or meal. No lovemaking. One of them kept watch over their hatching-to-be night and day, and many times it would be them both lying on the bed with the egg between them.

The day was drawing to a close and he gazed up at the sky. Twilight had descended and soon, the moon would rise, a pink cast covering it that would eventually turn blood red once midnight had passed and Valentine's Day officially arrived. The special moon was part of the Vale Valley magic, visible only to those who lived within the borders of the small town, a symbol of love to mark the special day.

Vic's mind was made up. They would share a meal at home, drink champagne and toast their love right there at their bedside where the egg lay safely tucked into the nest. It didn't matter where he gave Kellan the ring. His sweet swan would be thrilled no matter what.

Vic put the truck in gear and was about to back out of the parking space when his cell went off. He noted that it was Kellan calling. *I'm sure he's wondering what's taken me so long.*

He'd barely answered when Kellan's excited shout burst from the phone.

"Hurry, Vic! The egg has started to crack!"

The phone flew from his hand, his tires squealing as the truck lurched backward before he jetted down the street toward home.

He couldn't even remember whether he'd responded to Kellan or hung up.

Our baby. Our baby is almost here!

$\approx$

*A*vi and his medical team had arrived before Dr. Arthur, and Kellan assumed Vic was on his way too. He wasn't sure. After Vic had answered all he'd heard was a yell and a loud clunk which he assumed was Vic's phone slamming against something.

But regardless, it seemed as if half the town of Vale Valley was in the parking lot and surrounding their cabin. Avi stuck his head in the bedroom, since Kellan hadn't left the egg alone for one second. He'd had to shout for the fire department to let themselves in.

"Kellan? My uncle said he's on his way. I guess your phone has been busy. Also, there's a little cutie out here, says his name is Sean. He's very worried about you and the egg."

Kellan smiled at the handsome eagle shifter with the salt and pepper hair, his masculine face and bearing striking him as regal when they'd first met. He thought Dr. Arthur's nephew seemed perfect for the position of fire chief.

"He's my friend. Tell him we're okay, but I'm waiting until Vic and the doctor get here before I'll have any news. Your uncle told us that once the egg starts hatching that we can't have people around it because of germs and stuff."

Avi nodded. "I understand. Eagle eggs have the same issue. I'll pass the word along. Some staff from the restaurant have been trying to angle their way in too."

Kellan chuckled. "I'm sure you mean Dora and Skip. Tell everyone we'll keep them updated."

"Will do. If you need anything else before they get here, just holler."

"Thanks, Avi."

Once he'd left, Kellan returned his attention to the egg. *The crack is getting bigger*. Ever since he'd first realized their baby was on the way, that their little hatchling was trying to push their way out, he'd been trembling from the anticipation, but a thread of fear still nagged at him too. *Come on, sweetie. You can do it*. The possibility still existed that if the baby's wolf didn't know what to do or the hatching took too long, they'd have to take the egg to the hospital. He and Vic had already been warned about the risks involved in taking that route.

Raised voices could be heard near the front of the cabin, with Vic's bellowing tone overriding the others. Kellan let out a long, slow breath. *At last*. It had probably only been about fifteen minutes since he'd spoken to him, but he needed his mate by his side. Even though their baby was doing all the work, he wanted Vic there holding his hand in reassurance.

The door flew open and Vic covered his mouth as if he'd startled himself. With a whispered 'sorry', he softly closed the door behind him. He tiptoed over to the bed then leaned over.

"Is-is that it?" Vic pointed to the tiny line at the top of the egg that had gone from being about one inch long to close to three. His voice was still whisper soft and he'd kept the end of his finger well away from actually touching the shell.

"Yes, it is. And you don't have to whisper. I've been talking to the baby and encouraging him or her to come out."

"Oh, okay." Vic stared at the egg in wonder. "Should I do that too?"

"I think it's a good idea. You know, swan hatchlings imprint on the first people they see, so it's important that we're both here." Kellen tilted his head. "Do wolf babies do that too?"

Vic still hadn't taken his eyes off the egg. "Well, it's more about scent with wolves. But it can't hurt."

Vic tore his gaze away for barely a moment to grab the chair they kept in the bedroom and dragged it closer to the bed. Kellan frowned.

"Why are you doing that? Don't you want to be on the bed with us?" Kellan found himself becoming more emotional than seemed reasonable over such a small thing.

"That's okay? I don't want to hurt it or... I don't know." Vic ran his fingers through his hair, his nervousness palpable. "It just hit me how clueless I am about everything. I want to be the best mate and father I can be, but I'm afraid I'll screw it up."

"Oh, Vic." Kellan held out a hand to him. "Come sit with me." He knew it had to have been hard for his proud and resilient Alpha mate to admit to such a thing. "Just being here and loving us is all you need to do."

Vic accepted Kellan's hand then lowered himself gingerly onto the mattress. He placed an arm around Kellan's waist, pulling him closer until they were flush to each other.

"You're so brave, sweetheart. I'll always be here, protecting and loving you both. I promise."

They touched their heads together and watched the egg in silence. After a few minutes, the egg jerked twice and the crack not only got longer, but a tad wider. They both gasped and leaned forward, examining the new development.

"I can't see anything, just something filmy." Vic's brow was creased, and his eyes narrowed as he stared.

Kellan viewed the opening at different angles. "That's the membrane, but maybe we can see the baby—" He slapped a hand to his mouth then pointed. "There! Did you see that? I saw..." He wasn't a hundred percent sure *what* he saw, but it was something. "It might have been his hand, or maybe... an elbow?"

Vic arched his eyebrows as he regarded him. "His?"

Kellan shook his head, shrugging. "I don't know. It just flew out of my mouth."

The egg jerked some more, enough so that Kellan worried it might roll off the bed.

"Vic? You'd better—"

Before he'd completed the sentence, Vic had already rushed to the other side of the bed so that they were both framing the nest.

He let out a loud exhale. "Got it."

Kellan chewed on his lip. *Where's Dr. Arthur? He's taking forever.*

Every once in a while, Kellan and Vic would exchange glances, but for the most part, they kept their attention on the progress of their unborn child's attempt at hatching. Kellan plucked his phone from the nightstand, not only to check the time but to give Dr. Arthur another call. He let out a yelp and dropped the cell at the sound of a knock on the bedroom door.

"Who is it?"

Vic's voice held a no-nonsense tone. He clearly didn't want them to be disturbed either.

"It's Dr. Arthur."

Kellan slapped a hand to his chest. *Oh, thank gods.*

A low growl rumbled in Vic's chest. "Then come in."

As if in response to the doctor's arrival, a tiny bit of shell poked up from the top of the egg. Kellan's stomach clenched.

"Hurry!"

Dr. Arthur strolled into the room with a smile on his face as if there wasn't the most important thing in the world going on right then.

"Oh my." His smile broadened as he moved closer to the nest. "This is wonderful." He regarded Kellan. "When did the first crack appear?"

Kellan blinked several times as he willed his brain to work. He had nothing. Instead, he reached down to retrieve his phone from where it had landed on the rug. After checking the time, he answered the doctor, "Close to an hour ago."

Dr. Arthur's eyes widened. "Well, now. You have a very anxious baby. They're clearly ready to get out of that egg after all this time!"

Kellan wrung his hands. "That's good, right?"

Dr. Arthur had the nerve to chuckle when Kellan was so worried. "Very good. I'll check the heartbeat as well as the health of the membrane, but judging from the progress of the hatching so far, I'd say we're looking at only a few more hours."

Kellan bounced on the bed before catching himself when Vic gasped then grabbed the egg to steady it.

"Oops, sorry." Kellan petted the base of the egg. "Your daddy's just really excited to see you."

Vic let out a long exhale. "Just curious. How long do swan eggs usually take to hatch?"

Dr. Arthur was already removing his stethoscope from this bag. "Of course, it depends, but typically it's about twelve to fifteen hours." He placed the metal disc on the egg, then slowly moved it around the shell, pausing in different spots as he continued, "But I suspect that the combination of the wolf DNA and how long the baby has been incubating has sped up the progress." Dr. Arthur straightened. "This is a tough one you've got here, from the sounds of it. Not only do we have a strong heartbeat, but I can hear some small cries. They want out of there *bad*."

Kellan grinned. His fears were morphing into yet more excitement. "What should we be doing now? Anything else?"

"No hurry, but I'd at least make sure you have a clean basin so you can add warm water once the egg is open all the way and the membrane is off. That way, any residue can be cleaned off. Don't interfere with the membrane unless the baby can't get out of it themselves, since they'll need to be breathing air at that point." He chuckled. "Although, with this feisty one, it shouldn't be an issue. I'll head over to the inn, grab a bite and relax while we wait. Call me once the baby is here so I can give them a checkup, get them washed off and so on." He patted Kellan's shoulder. "Everything's fine. The only thing you can do is keep an eye on the egg and maybe get some blankets to wrap your new arrival in."

At last Kellan felt as if he could breathe. "Thank you, doctor. I appreciate it." He drew his eyebrows together. "And we can't have anyone else in here until they're hatched, right?"

"Correct. I'll let the excited crowd that's gathered outside know they can go about their business for now." He winked then left the room.

Kellan turned to Vic, tears springing to his eyes at the expression of pure love he saw there. Their family was about to expand,

and he no longer held any doubt that Vic was filled with the same joy as he. Kellan returned his gaze to their egg, picturing in his mind the moment when they would get the first glimpse of the new addition to their family.

Of our sweet baby.

CHAPTER SEVEN

*V*ic's eyes burned from staring at the egg, afraid to blink in case the baby burst free of the shell and he missed the moment. Logically, he knew such a thing was ridiculous, yet he couldn't tear his gaze away. He'd almost pissed himself earlier because he'd been so afraid to leave the egg. When Kellan had noticed him wiggling around, he'd ordered Vic to use the bathroom, reassuring him that he'd remain wrapped around the base of the egg so it didn't jettison off the bed.

He and Kellan barely spoke, and when they did, it was with hushed words. Kellan had dimmed the lamp some more and the curtains were drawn, although the light from outside had ceased to be an issue for quite a while. Kellan had also instructed him on where all the necessary items were located to use for the baby's arrival. The bulb to clear the baby's airway, the layette, clean towels and the basin to put water in. He checked the time again and noted that barely five minutes had passed since the last time he'd looked.

Ten minutes to midnight. He was going crazy.

Most of the top of the egg was cracked and while they could see the top of the baby's head as he or she twisted inside the confines of the shell, they remained curled up so their face was never visible. The suspense was killing him.

"Sweetheart? You must be hungry. If you wrap yourself around the egg again, I can go make something for you to eat."

He didn't want to leave the room for a second, but he didn't want his poor mate to suffer either. As if on cue, his own stomach rumbled. *Hmm. I guess I'm starting to feel it too.*

Kellan regarded him with a wrinkled brow. "I don't know. My stomach is in knots."

"Yeah, me too." Vic offered him a smile. "But when's the last time you had anything?"

Kellan sighed. "Around noon."

Vic nodded. "So basically, the last time I ate too."

Kellan gave him a sheepish smile. "I guess you're right. Maybe only some fruit, though? I don't think I can handle much else."

He wasn't sure how much he could choke down either, but his wolf was *not* pleased with him.

"I'll be quick. But yell if anything happens."

He gave Kellan a quick kiss then headed to the kitchen. He chopped up some apples and pears, then added some cheese, just in case. Kellan didn't eat much of it but would on occasion. With as nervous as his stomach was, Vic didn't think he could handle getting into Kellan's secret stash that held all the 'unique' cuisine he favored. He'd accidentally opened a canister on the counter one day and discovered that his mate also ate things with antennas, segmented eyes and wings that were not related to birds in any way.

Vic made up a similar plate for himself but added a couple slices of cold ham. He also added two bottles of cold water to the tray. Once he'd gotten to the kitchen, he'd realized that they both hadn't been drinking anything either. Deciding that the snack and water should hold them until the baby arrived, he carried it back to the room.

The moment Vic passed the threshold the tray hit the floor with a clatter. Kellan was on his knees, both hands held to his mouth, his eyes rounded as if in shock. Vic knew how he felt. His jaw dropped as he gaped at the wolf pup clawing its way out of the gooey membrane, the bottom half of him or her still hidden inside the base of the egg.

His brain couldn't process what he was seeing. Wolf shifters weren't born in wolf form. And even when they did shift, it didn't occur until puberty. Was their child okay? Vic moved toward the bed to take a closer look.

A white wolf.

"Dr. Arthur," Kellan's voice croaked out. "C-call Dr. Arthur."

"Yeah." Vic continued to stare as their baby wriggled free of the egg sac. "Good plan." He remained frozen.

"Vic! The doctor!"

He jerked his head in Kellan's direction. "Huh? Oh shit! Right."

Vic's hand shook as he retrieved the cell from his pocket. Thankfully, he had the doctor's phone number programmed in. Pressing one button was about as much as his addled brain could handle.

"Hello? Dr. Arthur, you have to—oh fuck!"

Vic dropped the phone and rushed to Kellan's side as their white baby wolf shifted into a fuzzy, albeit wet, grey and black cygnet.

They turned to face each other, their mouths open in silent shock. They went back to staring at their wobbly swan baby as it tried to get its webbed feet under itself before collapsing again. It had managed to get completely free of the shell and was clearly breathing okay, so Vic took that much as a good sign. They both moved closer to the cygnet who was about twice the size of a typical swan baby, their faces only a foot away from their newborn.

Their baby let out a series of small chirps as it gazed up at them, opening and closing its beak and making a weak attempt to flap its wings.

Kellan whimpered, "I want to hold him."

"Clean him off and let me give him the once over. Then you can." Dr. Arthur's voice startled them out of their reverie.

Kellan's words began to tumble out. "He came out as a white wolf, right out of the egg just like that and then he shifted to a cygnet and now he's still—well, you can see he's still a cygnet, that's obvious—but he hasn't been a regular baby yet and I'm scared something's wrong and I don't know if he should eat pureed snails when he's a wolf or what's going on..." Kellan ended his ramblings on a wail.

Dr. Arthur moved around to the other side of the bed. "Now, now Kellan. Your little one is strong and breathing well. First thing's first." The doctor regarded Vic. "Can you get me some warm water, not too hot." He returned his attention to Kellan. "No matter what, you have what seems to be a healthy child. I'll be with you both through this new journey. Remember, inter-species shifter children aren't that unusual. Just because this is a new one on me, doesn't mean there's anything wrong with your child, all right?"

Kellan sniffed. "All right."

Dr. Arthur arched his eyebrows at Vic and he remembered he was supposed to be getting the water instead of standing there doing nothing. Once he'd returned, the baby had gone back to wolf form. His heart clutched at the sight of Kellan crying. The helplessness Vic felt at not being able to fix everything for his mate cut through him.

"Here you go, doc."

They both remained transfixed on the scene before them as Dr. Arthur wiped their child clean, checked their airways and heartbeat then wrapped them in a blanket. He smiled at Kellan, offering the squirming, yipping bundle to him.

"Here's your baby."

Kellan 'ooohed' as he accepted their newborn, staring with awe at them. Vic sat on the bed and moved closer to his mate so he could see better. He furrowed his brow, scenting the air.

"I think... I think the baby is a boy."

Kellan smiled up at him. "I think so too. I don't know why, but it felt that way earlier too."

Vic smiled back and kissed his forehead. He gazed down at the wolf pup still struggling and mewling in Kellan's arms.

"Welcome, baby Erik."

"Yes, little Erik." Kellan looked at him again. "Are you disappointed that he's part-swan, that he's not...like a regular baby?" Kellan's lip trembled.

"No, sweetheart, not at all. As long as he's healthy, that's all I care about. He's my son and I love him, no matter what."

Kellan nodded. "Me too. I only wanted to make sure you're happy."

Vic draped an arm around Kellan's shoulders and gave him a squeeze. "I'm thrilled. Don't you doubt that for a second."

Dr. Arthur interjected, "I don't think there's anything else I can do right now, so I'm going to grab some sleep. My nephew has invited me to spend the night in his guest room. Bit of a long drive for me this time of night, and I want you to bring little Erik to Vale General tomorrow. I'll give you a call in the morning with the time. I'll have to arrange it with their obstetrician who handles male pregnancies."

Vic rose to escort Dr. Arthur to the door, thanking him for all his help. By the time he'd returned to their bedroom, he could tell how exhausted Kellan was, and he had to admit that he was feeling rather tired himself. The adrenaline of the day had exacted a toll on them both and Vic thought is was advisable that they at least try to get some sleep.

"Vic? I think he's hungry. We have the special shifter baby formula in the cupboard. Since he's a wolf right now, maybe we can try it?"

He'd warned Kellan that wolf shifters didn't shift until much later, so they hadn't taken the possibility of having a pup in consideration. "We're in such unknown territory right now that I think we should give it a try. We don't want him to go hungry. I'll go prepare some."

"Thanks, Vic."

As he left the room, he smiled at the sounds of Kellan cooing and talking to their baby. Wolf or swan or both—Vic loved their child with all his heart.

∼

*K*ellan couldn't keep his eyes open. They kept fluttering closed and even though he had the baby —who had changed back into a swan—on a nest of new blankets between him and Vic, he didn't want to go to sleep, just in case. In case *what*, he wasn't sure, but staying awake was his main objective.

So far, little Erik had taken about a quarter of a bottle of shifter formula without spitting it up, then after he'd peed in his old nest, he'd drifted off to sleep. His shift back to a swan had happened with minimal fuss before he'd tucked his head under his wing and settled down again.

Vic snorted and snuffled, his interrupted snore apparently rousing him. He rubbed his knuckles over his eyes from where he lay on his back. He yawned then rolled on his side.

"When did he change again?"

Kellan sighed as he gazed down at their son. "About an hour ago, around four."

Vic furrowed his brow. "Have you had *any* sleep?"

Kellan shook his head. "I can't. I don't want to miss anything. What if he needs me?"

With a smile, Vic reached across the blankets below the nest and clasped Kellan's fingers. "You're such a good daddy. But you'll make yourself sick if you don't get some rest and that won't help Erik either. Why don't I sit with him a while so you can close your eyes and take a break?"

"I don't know..." He was exhausted, but it seemed wrong somehow. *But Vic will be watching him.* "Okay. But wake me up if anything happens?"

"Of course, sweetheart." Vic's eyes widened a fraction. "I just realized something."

Kellan inclined his head. "What?"

Vic broke into a grin. "Happy Valentine's Day."

Kellan's chest filled with warmth. "Oh, Vic. Happy Valentine's Day, our very first one."

"First of many. You know what else?"

"What?"

"Erik is a Valentine's baby. He was fully hatched after midnight.

With a satisfied smile, Kellan snuggled against his pillow, facing their little shifter with Vic still holding his hand. His eyes fluttered and before another thought had the chance to form, he was asleep.

*R*esisting the urge to pet the downy covering of the cygnet wasn't easy. Thankfully, Kellan had been asleep for two hours, and although the grey light of dawn had begun to filter beneath the curtains, the room remained dark except for a small nightlight in the shape of a swan plugged into the wall.

The nap Vic had taken was wearing off and drowsiness was beginning to take hold again. He'd been teased already by everyone at work about what it would be like once the baby arrived, that he could wave goodbye to a full night's sleep for a while. Despite his concerns regarding their hatchling, he didn't regret a thing. Having a family—a true one—was worth any sacrifice. Even when things turned out differently than they would've wished, they were in it for the long haul.

Some frantic wiggling started up next to him and he figured Erik might have shifted back to a wolf and be ready to eat again. Instead, when he glanced down, he was met with the hooded eyes of a tiny person. Not a wolf. Not a swan. A regular baby.

Yup. Definitely a boy.

Right as he was about to wake Kellan up, the baby did it for him by letting out a piercing wail. With a start, Kellan jerked to a sitting position.

"Wha—what's happening?"

Vic turned on the nightstand lamp so they could both get a good look at their screaming newborn.

"See for yourself, sweetheart." Vic grinned at the sight of Kellan cooing at and cuddling their clearly infuriated baby.

"Vic, can you get some more formula? And a diaper?"

The baby continued struggling, his arms waving around and his legs going *kick, kick, kick* as his face turned red from his lusty cries and Kellan fought to get him wrapped in a blanket.

From Vic's point of view the diaper was the more urgent item to retrieve. They would run out of blankets in no time otherwise. After he'd handed one to Kellan, he hurried to the kitchen to make more formula for his son.

My son.

He teared up as a wave of emotion washed over him. A year ago he'd been going through the motions, having long given up on ever having his true mate—let alone a child. The gods had blessed him with the most perfect and beautiful mate and now, with a sweet, healthy child. He had all he'd ever wanted.

His son wasn't getting any quieter and clearly uninterested in his father's sentimental musings.

After checking the temperature of the formula with a few drops on his wrist, he carried the bottle into the bedroom. He handed it to Kellan but couldn't tear his gaze from his baby.

"Closer. I can't reach, Vic."

"Huh?" He reluctantly looked away and realized Kellan was stretching as far as he could to get the bottle Vic still gripped. "Oh, gods. Sorry."

He placed their baby's breakfast into Kellan's open hand then traveled to the other side of the bed so he could climb in and join them. Vic released a satisfied sigh as he watched Kellan feed their now-contented infant, his strong and steady pull on the nipple of the bottle yet more reassurance that all was well with their child.

Now that he's awake, I can touch all I want without bothering him. Vic figured that was the case, but it still felt like he was about to touch a delicate piece of crystal. He used one finger to pet Eric's head. *So soft.* He narrowed his eyes as he studied the fine strands of hair lying flat against his baby's scalp.

"Kellan, look. He has a patch of pure white hair over here, black across the top then some grey down the other side. I thought the white was his scalp, but it's actually hair."

"You're right." Kellan inspected Erik as well. "He really is made up of both of us."

Vic pressed his lips to Kellan's temple. "He certainly is."

Vic scooted closer to his mate and child, wrapping an arm around Kellan's shoulders so they could lean against each other. Kellan adjusted their little bundle so that Erik's head remained in the crook of his arm and his feet rested on Vic's lap.

In that moment, Vic knew everything would be fine.

EPILOGUE

*S*pring had arrived and so had the day of his marriage to Vic. Kellan wore all white—an untucked silk shirt and flat front dress slacks, a gentle breeze blowing off the lake catching the sheer fabric of the top and making it shimmer from the sun. He glanced at his empty ring finger, the stunning platinum ring Vic had given him the day after Erik had been born waiting in Vic's jacket pocket to soon be placed where it belonged.

Big, fluffy clouds broke up the bright blue backdrop of the sky and Kellan was glad they'd waited until May to hold their wedding. As recently as two weeks before it had still been raining quite regularly.

But now it's time.

Kellan stood by the bench he'd sat on with Vic to watch a winter sunset over the lake on one of their first dates. Sweet Bites was catering the reception which was being held back at the restaurant, and Skip was only mildly butthurt that he hadn't been put in charge of the food. However, the true magic was how gorgeous the setting was for their special day.

Dora, Lena and her wife, Sue, had been in charge of putting together the floral archway he and Vic would be married under, arranging the white folding chairs in a semi-circle with an aisle in the center and placing the flowers in and around the staging area. They had used a combination of white roses, ferns and Kellan's favorite flower of all time—tulips.

"Are you ready?" Dora ambled up to him, strolling baby Erik who was snoozing in the carrier that could be removed from the stroller part, if necessary.

Kellan gazed down at his sleeping child. "Do you have enough formula to last through the wedding? Is there more at the restaurant? What about the jars of pureed meal worms, venison and peaches?"

"Umm, can we not talk about that right now? And yes, I have that, a bottle of water, more diapers, and whatever else you've stuffed in this enormous bag hanging from the handle of the stroller." She sighed. "And you didn't answer my question. Vic's on his way over from the cabin with Skip and it looks like most of the chairs are filled." She pointed to the archway. "Even Father Lance has taken his place at the altar."

A smile stretched across Kellan's face at the realization that he wasn't nervous. Excited, definitely. But how could he be anything but thrilled when he was about to pledge himself to his fated mate?

"I'm ready."

Dora threw her arms around him. "I'm so glad I met you and we became friends. I love you, Kellan. You're the best."

Kellan's face flushed hot. "I love you too, Dora. Thank you for everything."

She framed his face with her palms. "You are so adorable, I just want to eat you up."

He twisted out of her hold. "Stop. Am not."

Dora jerked her head in the direction of Sean, who had

settled into Vale Valley nicely. The shy young man was leaning against a tree behind the rows of chairs. Sean had also filled the gap at the restaurant that Kellan had left behind now that he was a fulltime parent. Kellan was more grateful than Sean would ever know. The guilt over telling everyone he wouldn't be going back had been epic.

"Then there's that one over there. I think he's lonely. You should introduce him to someone."

Kellan's eyes widened. "Me? I don't know anyone. And he told me he likes staying in his room, that it's peaceful."

Dora snorted. "That's ridiculous. Both to him staying in his room and you not knowing anyone. Everyone you meet is your friend."

Once Dora got going on a subject, it was difficult to move her off it. Kelan spotted a good opportunity.

"Look, here comes Vic and Skip now. Did Skip forget to wear his tie? I don't want him ruining the wedding pics."

Dora spotted them and gasped. "What the hell does he think he's doing?" She pressed her lips in a tight line. "Don't worry, Kellan. I'm on it." She started marching toward them, pushing his sleeping baby in the stroller with purpose. "Hey! Skip! Don't you walk away from me."

Kellan chuckled behind his hand. He hoped her onslaught didn't delay the wedding too much, but he'd wanted a few moments to himself before going down the aisle. Not to mention wanting to avoid the subject of Sean's social life. Kellan knew better than anyone what Sean had endured at the hands of his brother and ex-herd, and if he wanted to keep to himself for a while, Kellan didn't blame him at all. It certainly didn't help that the shifter network hadn't captured Finn yet.

With a happy sigh, Kellan took in the view of the surroundings once more. Soon, Lena would be playing a song from the *Nutcracker Suite* on her classical guitar, which would then be his cue to walk down the aisle. After some pondering, he'd decided to go down the aisle alone. He'd never had a father figure, had never had a mentor. As a young swan he'd lost the part of his family who had loved and cared about him and his life had been hell until he'd been rescued by Vic—both literally and figuratively. He would walk to his mate and offer his heart to him for all time. No one else deserved to be a part of that sacred moment, no one had the right to give him away.

As soon as Vic and Skip—who now wore a tie—had taken their places at the altar, a hush seemed to descend over the crowd. Only the gentle lapping of the water at the edges of the lake and the musical chirping of songbirds could be heard surrounding them. Lena, dressed in a flowing, three-quarter length dress of white and a bold pattern of lavender lilies, approached the front with her guitar, then stood on what would be Kellan's side of the altar.

The first gentle strains of the guitar rang out and, after taking a deep breath, Kellan retrieved his simple bouquet from the park bench—a bundle of white tulips tied together with a satin ribbon. Happy tears sprang to his eyes as he took confident steps toward his mate and best friend.

Kellan reached the front right as Lena had finished the song, exactly as they'd rehearsed it. He handed his bouquet to her then took Vic's outstretched hand.

This is it. In a few minutes, I'm going to be Vic's husband.

He tried not to bounce on his toes.

Father Lance offered them a warm smile. "It is with great joy that I welcome you all here on this beautiful day to celebrate the marriage of Kellan Rivers and Vic Russo. In the time I've come to know them, I have witnessed the love, friendship and support they share with each other. No two people deserve to be united in matrimony more than these men."

A cry erupted right as Father Lance had taken a breath to

continue. A low murmur rose from the onlookers and Kellan whipped his head around in search of Erik. He'd recognize that cry anywhere. He turned to Vic with pleading eyes, but instead of rebuke, he was met with his mate's understanding smile.

Kellan went up on his toes and whispered in his ear. "I'll be right back."

Vic squeezed his hands then let go. "And I'll be right here waiting. I would wait forever for you."

Kellan sniffed, wiping a finger under one eye as he scurried to get their child. Ever since that first week when Erik would shift back and forth between swan, wolf and baby, they both had been over-protective parents. Their baby rarely shifted now, which was more in line with the average shifter baby. Since Erik was still an anomaly to the shifter medical community, they could only guess as to why he'd come into the world the way he had. Dr. Arthur's theory was that he'd been trying to instinctually unite all his different sides.

Once Kellan had retrieved his sobbing infant and Dora had handed him a bottle, Kellan rejoined his mate at the altar. Together, they exchanged vows, all while Kellan cradled their firstborn.

Firstborn. Kellan smiled, his heart happier and lighter than he'd ever dared dream. He had the feeling Erik would be the first of many.

MORE VALE VALLEY FROM M.M. WILDE

Sean finds his Happily-Ever-After in Vale Valley's summer
season with
A Swan's Love Song

True love is the only magic Sean has ever wished for...

After being rescued from a vicious gang of thieving swans by
fellow swan shifter Kellan, Sean is starting over in the magical
town of Vale Valley. Despite being so young, he aches to find his
Alpha so he can begin his forever after. And once he's spent lots
of time with Kellan and Vic's adorable hatchling, he also dreams
of having an egg of his very own.

Avi is Vale Valley's recently hired fire chief and an eagle shifter.
He can't keep his eyes off the blond cutie who's a server at the
Vale Valley Inn restaurant, but he's so busy with his job. In addition, he's much older than the delectable Sean. Avi decides he
should probably just behave and keep his wings to himself.

Sometimes all a fated mate needs is a swift kick in the ass. When Sean repeatedly fails to convince Avi they were meant to be, he enlists the help of his new friends. Too bad there's an old enemy skulking around who can't wait to ruin everything...

ALSO BY M.M. WILDE

Rescued by the Alpha (Alaskan Wolf Alliance 1)

When wishing for a new life, Elam finds out the hard way he should've been more specific.

A year in the Alaskan wilderness was supposed to help nature photographer Elam start over. However, hitting his head and being rescued by one of the hottest men he's laid eyes on in a while is not getting him off to a great start. Elam had promised himself he'd stay away from sexy guys after his rat of an ex cheated on him.

Nicolai is a rare, blue-eyed white wolf shifter. He's also an Alpha and the expected heir to his pack in the Alaskan Wolf Alliance. Much to his father's dismay, Nic has stepped aside as ruler and ceded his spot as future head of the pack. As a gay shifter, he refuses to claim a female omega for the sole purpose of providing a child to carry on the family line. However, fate intervenes and puts Nic on a collision course with a human mate.

When chemistry, love and the shock of what the growly Nic is blindsides Elam, he has some tough decisions to make. Does he let Nic turn him? Never go back to his old home? But the biggest surprise is yet to be revealed when Nic and Elam discover the new life Elam had hoped for is more than just his own—and that there are wolves frothing at the mouth to destroy it.

Rescued by the Alpha is Book One in the Alaskan Wolf Alliance series and features an Alpha and omega who are fated to have lots of steamy, knotty fun and to make beautiful babies together. This romantic tale with a dose of action and suspense does include some peril to Dad and baby. But, there's a fluffy, feel-good HEA and we all know wolves don't cheat, so no worries there!

ABOUT THE AUTHOR

M.M. Wilde is the knotty mpreg romance alter-ego of Morticia Knight, who loves all things strange and unusual. To keep up with the latest in releases, exclusive excerpts, cover reveals and the occasional giveaway—when M.M. is feeling particularly saucy—follow her on Twitter or Facebook. Need more mpreg? Then join the Special Delivery Mpreg Reader Group on Facebook, featuring M.M. Wilde, Michael Mandrake, Giovanna Reaves and L.M. Brown.

Manufactured by Amazon.ca
Bolton, ON

16037368R00120